The Swor

Marion Zimmer Bradley

COPYRIGHT

Marion Zimmer Bradley Literary Works Trust
PO Box 193473
San Francisco, CA 94119-3473
www.mzbworks.com

CHAPTER ONE

We were outstripping the night. The *Southern Cross* had made planetfall on Darkover at midnight. There I had embarked on the Terran skyliner that was to take me halfway around a planet; only an hour had passed, but already the thin air was beginning to flush red with a hint of dawn. Under my feet the floor of the big plane tilted slightly as it began to fly aslant down the western ridge of the Hellers. Peak after peak fell away astern, cutting the sparse clouds that capped the snowline; and already my memory was looking for landmarks, although I knew we were too high.

After six years of knocking around half a dozen star-systems, I was going home again; but I felt nothing. Not homesick. Not excited. Not even resentful. I hadn't wanted to return to Darkover, but I hadn't even cared enough to refuse.

Six years ago I had left Darkover, intending never to return. The Regent's desperate message had followed me from Terra, to Samarra, to Vainwal. It costs plenty to send a personal message interspace, even over the Terran relay system, and Old Hastur—Regent of the Comyn, Lord of the Seven Domains—hadn't wasted words in explaining. It had simply been a command. But I couldn't imagine why they wanted me back. They'd all been glad to see the last of me, when I went

I turned from the paling light at the window, closing my eyes and pressing my good hand to my temple. The interstellar passage, as always, had been made under heavy sedation. Now the dope that the ship's medic had given me was beginning to wear off; fatigue cut down my barriers, letting in a teasing telepathic trickle of thought.

I could *feel* the covert stares of the other passengers, at my scarred face, at the arm that ended at the wrist in a folded sleeve, but mostly at *what* and *who* I was. A telepath. A freak. An Alton—one of the Seven Families of the Comyn—that hereditary autarchy which has ruled Darkover since long before our sun faded to red.

And yet, not quite one of them. My father, Kennard Alton—every child on Darkover could repeat the story—had done a shocking, almost a shameful thing. He had married, taken in honorable *laran* marriage, a Terran woman, kin to the hated Empire people who have overrun the civilized Galaxy.

He had been powerful enough to brazen it out. They had needed my father in Comyn Council. After Old Hastur, he had been the most powerful man in the Comyn. He'd even managed to cram me down their throats. But they'd all been glad when I left Darkover. And now I had come home.

In the seat in front of me, two professorish-looking Earthmen, probably research workers on holiday from mapping and exploring, were debating the old chestnut of origins. One was stubbornly defending the theory of parallel evolutions; the other, the theory that some ancient planet—preferably Earth itself—colonized the whole Galaxy a million years ago. I concentrated on their conversation, trying to shut out awareness of the stares around me. Telepaths are never at ease in crowds.

The Dispersionist brought out all the old arguments for a lost age of star-travel, and the other man was arguing about the nonhuman races and the differing levels of culture on any single planet.

"Darkover, for instance," he argued. "A planet still in early feudal culture, trying to reconcile itself to the impact of the Terran empire—"

I lost interest. It was amazing, how many Terrans still thought of Darkover as a feudal or barbarian planet. Simply because we retain, not resistance, but indifference to Terran imports of machinery and weapons; because we prefer to ride horses and mules, as an ordinary thing, rather than spend our time in building roads. And because Darkover, bound by the ancient Compact, wants to take no chance of a return to the days of war and mass murder with coward's weapons. That is the law on all planets of the Darkovan League, and all civilized worlds outside. Who would kill, must come within reach of death. They could talk disparagingly of the code duello and the feudal system. I'd heard it all, on Terra. But isn't it more civilized to kill your personal enemy at hand-grips, with sword or knife, than to slay a thousand strangers at a safe distance?

The people of Darkover have held out, better than most, against the glamour of the Terran Empire. I've been on other planets, and I've seen what happened to most worlds when the Earthmen come in with the lure of a civilization that spans the stars. They don't subdue new worlds by force of arms. The Earthmen can afford to sit back and wait until the native culture simply collapses under their impact. They wait till the planet begs to be taken into the Empire. And sooner or later the planet does—and becomes one more link in the vast, over-centralized monstrosity swallowing world after world.

It hadn't happened here, not yet.

A man near the front of the cabin rose and made his way toward me; without permission, he swung himself into the empty seat at my side.

"Comyn?" But it wasn't a question.

The man was tall and sparely built: mountain Darkovan, Cahuenga from the Hellers. His stare dwelt, an instant past politeness, on the scars and the empty sleeve; then he nodded.

"I thought so," he said. "You were the boy who was mixed up in that Sharra business."

I felt the blood rise in my face. I had spent six years forgetting the Sharra rebellion—and Marjorie Scott. I would bear the scars forever. Who the hell was this man, to remind me?

"Whatever I was," I said curtly. "I am not, now. And I don't remember you."

"And you an Alton!" he mocked lightly.

"In spite of all scare stories," I said, "Altons don't go around casually reading minds. In the first place, it's hard work. In the second place most people's minds are too full of muck. And in the third place," I added, "we just don't give a damn."

He laughed. "I didn't expect you to recognize me," he said. "You were drugged and delirious when I saw you last. I told your father that hand would have to come off eventually. I'm sorry I was right about it." He didn't sound sorry at all. "I'm Dyan Ardais."

Now I remembered him, after a fashion, a mountain lord from the far fastnesses of the Hellers. There had never been any love lost, even in the Comyn, between the Altons and the men of the Ardais.

"You travel alone? Where is your father, young Alton?"

"My father died on Vainwal," I said shortly.

His voice was a purr. "Then welcome, *Comyn* Alton!" The ceremonial title was a shock as he spoke it. He glanced at the square of paling window.

"We're coming in to Thendara. Will you travel with me?"

"I expect to be met." I didn't, but I had no wish to prolong this chance acquaintance. Dyan bowed, unruffled. "We shall meet in Council," he said, and added, with lazy elegance, "Oh, and guard your belongings well, *Comyn* Alton. There are, doubtless, some who would like to recover the Sharra matrix."

He spun round and walked away and I sat slack, in shock. Damn! Had he picked my mind as I sat there? *How else had he known?* The dirty Cahuenga! Still doped with procalamin as I was, he could have gotten inside my telepathic barriers and out again before I knew it. *But would one of the Comyn stoop so far?*

I stared after him, furiously; started to rise, and fell back with a jolt; we were losing altitude rapidly. The sign flashed to fasten seat belts; I fumbled at mine, my mind in turmoil.

He had forced memory on me—forced me to remember *why* I had left Darkover six years ago, scarred and broken and maimed for life. Wounds that had begun to heal, with time and silence, tore at me again. And he had spoken the name of Sharra.

A half-caste boy, a bastard, Comyn by special grace only because my father had no Darkovan sons, I had been easy prey for the rebels and malcontents swarming under the rallying cry of *Sharra*. Sharra—the legend called her a goddess turned daemon, bound in golden chains, called forth by fire. I had stood at those fires, using my telepath gifts to summon forth the powers of Sharra.

The Aldarans, the Comyn family exiled for dealing with the Terrans, had been at the center of the rebellion. I was a kinsman of Beltran, Lord of Aldaran.

Faces I had tried to forget marched relentlessly out to torment me. The man called Kadarin, rebel extraordinary, who had persuaded me to join the rebels of Sharra. The Scotts: drunken Zeb Scott who had found the talisman matrix of Sharra, and his children. Little Rafe, who had followed me about, his hero; Thyra, with the face of a girl and the eyes of a wild beast. And Marjorie...

Marjorie! Time slid away. A frightened girl with soft brown hair and gold-flecked amber eyes stole to my side through the strange firelight. Laughing, she walked the streets of a city that was now smashed rubble, a garland of golden flowers in her hand....

I slammed the memory shut. That wouldn't help. The thrum of the braking jets hurt my ears; out the window I could see the stubby towers of Thendara, rosy in the pink sunlight: a bright spot on the dark plains, patched with forests and low hills. We dipped lower and lower, and I saw lakes flash like silver mirrors; then the skyscraper peak of the Terran HQ building flashed past the window, the glare and whiteness of the spaceport struck my eyes, there was a jar, and a bump, and we were down. I tore at my straps. Now for Dyan—

But I missed him. The airfield was a scrabble of humans from thirty planets, jabbering in a hundred languages, and as I pushed my way through the crowd, I ran with smashing force into a thin girl dressed in white.

She stumbled and fell, and I bent to help her to her feet. "Please forgive me," I said in Standard, "I should have been looking where I was going—" and then I got a good look at her.

"Linnell!" I cried out joyfully, "by all that's wonderful!" I caught her up clumsily, hugging her. "Did you come to meet me? But, little cousin, how you've grown!"

"I beg your pardon!" The girl's voice was dripping with ice.

Suddenly aghast, I set her on her feet. She was speaking Darkovan now, but no Darkovan girl ever had such an accent. I stared at her, appalled.

"I'm sorry," I said at last, dumbfounded. "I thought—" but I kept on staring. She was a tall girl, very fair, with a soft heart-shaped face and soft dark brown hair and gentle gray eyes—but they were not gentle now; they were blazing with anger.

"Well?"

"I'm sorry," I repeated numbly, "I thought you were one of my cousins."

She gave a cool shrug, murmured something and moved away. I followed her with my eyes, still staring. The resemblance was fantastic. It wasn't just a superficial similarity of coloring and height; the girl was a mirror image of my cousin, Linnell Aillard. Even her voice sounded like Linnell's.

A light hand touched my shoulder and a gay girlish voice said, "Shame, Lew! How you must have embarrassed poor Linnell! She brushed past me without even speaking! Have you been away so long that you have forgotten all your manners?"

"Dio Ridenow!" I said, startled.

The girl beside me was small and pert, with flaxen-gold hair fluttering about her shoulders, and her green-gray eyes were aslant with mischief. "I thought you were on Vainwal," I said.

"And when you said good-bye to me there, you thought I would stay alone to cry my eyes out," she said saucily. "Not I! The space lanes are free to women as well as men, Lew Alton, and I, too, have a place in Comyn Council, when I choose to take it. Why should I stay there and sleep alone?" She giggled. "Oh, Lew, you should see your face! What's the matter?"

"It wasn't Linnell," I said, and Dio stared.

"Who, then?" She looked around, but the girl who looked like Linnell had vanished into the crowds. "And where is my uncle? Have you quarreled with your father again, Lew?"

"No!" I said roughly. "He died on Vainwal!" *Didn't* anyone *on Darkover know it yet?* "Do you think anything less would bring me back here?"

I saw the mirth go out of Dio's face. "Oh, Lew! I'm sorry! I didn't know!"

She touched my arm again, but I shied away from her sympathy. Dio Ridenow was high explosive where I was concerned. On Vainwal, that had all been very well. But I knew, if she didn't, how quickly that old affair could flare up into passion again. I had troubles enough without woman trouble, too.

Once again I had failed to barricade my thoughts. Dio's fair face etched itself with crimson; and abruptly, catching her teeth in her lip, she turned and almost ran toward the spaceport barriers.

"Dio!" I called after her, but at that moment someone shouted my name.

And right there, I made my first mistake. I didn't go after her—don't ask me why. But someone called my name again.

"Lew! Lew Alton!"

And the next moment a slender, dark-haired boy in Terran clothing was smiling up at me.

"Lew! Welcome home!"

And I couldn't remember his name to save my life.

He looked familiar. He knew me, and I knew him. But I stood warily back, remembering how I had *recognized* Linnell. The youngster laughed.

"Don't you know me?"

"I've been away too long to be sure about anybody," I said. I reached for telepathic contact, but the drug was still fuzzing my brain; I sensed only the fringes of familiarity. I shook my head at the kid. He'd have been only a child when I left Darkover; he was still so young that I don't think he'd started shaving yet.

"Zandru's hells," I said, "you *couldn't* be Marius, could you?"

"Couldn't I?"

I still couldn't believe it. My brother Marius, the younger brother who had cost our Terran mother her life—could I possibly fail to recognize my own brother?

He was grinning up at me shyly, and I relaxed. "I'm sorry, Marius," I said. "You were so young, and you've changed so much. Well—"

"We can talk later," he said quickly. "You have to go through customs, and all, but I wanted to get to you first. What's the matter, Lew? You look funny. Sick?"

I leaned hard for a minute on his suddenly-steadying arm, until the vertigo had passed. "Procalamin," I said ruefully, and at his blank look elucidated. "They shoot us full of it, on starships, so we can take the hyperdrive stresses without coming apart at the seams. It takes a while to wear off, and I'm allergic to the stuff anyhow."

I caught his sideways glance, and my face grew grimmer. "Do I look that bad? That's right, you haven't seen me, have you, since I lost my hand and got my face cut up. Well, get a good look."

His eyes slid away, and I tightened my arm around his shoulders.

"I don't mind you staring," I said more gently, "but damned if I want you sneaking a look at me when you think I won't notice, because I always do. See?"

He relaxed and studied me frankly for a minute, then grinned. "Not pretty, but you never were much of a beauty, as I remember. Let's go."

I looked past the skyscraper of the HQ, and the tall buildings of the Trade City. Beyond them rose the vast, splintered teeth of the mountains; and poised far above the plain, the loom of the Comyn Castle, topped by the tall spire of the Keeper's Tower.

"Are the Comyn already assembled in Thendara?"

Marius shook his head. I still couldn't get used to the notion that this was my brother. He didn't *feel* right. "No," he said, "They—we're meeting out in the Hidden City. Lew, did you bring any guns from Terra?"

"Hell, no. What would I want with guns? And they're contraband anyhow."

"Then you're not armed at all."

I shook my head. "No. It's not allowed to carry side arms on most Empire planets and I've lost the habit. Why?"

He scowled. "I managed to get one last year," he said. "I paid four times what it was worth, and it has the contraband mark on it. I thought—wait, that's your name they're calling."

It was. I went slowly toward the low white customs building, Marius trailing after me. He shook his head at the officer on duty, and went on through. My luggage had been laid on the conveyer belt, and the clerk glanced at me without much interest.

"Lewis Alton-Kennard-Montray-Alton? Landed at Port Chicago on the *Southern Cross*? Matrix technician?"

I admitted all of it and showed the plastic chip which held my certification as a licensed matrix mechanic.

"We'll have to check this on the main banks," the Terran clerk said. "It will take an hour or two. We'll get in touch with you."

The clerk flicked his eyes over a printed form.

"Do - you - solemnly - affirm - that - to - the - best - of - your - knowledge - and - belief - you - have - not - in - your - possession - any - power - or - propulsion - weapons - guns - disintegrators - or - blasters - atomic - isotopes - narcotic - drugs - intoxicants - or - incendiaries?"

I signed. He hefted my luggage under the clarifier; the screen stayed blank, as I'd known it would. The items named were all items of Terran manufacture; by solemn compact with the Hasturs, the Empire is committed not to let them be brought into the Darkovan Zone, or anywhere outside the Trade Cities. Such items, contraband on our planet, were treated before they were brought here with a small speck of radioactive substance, harmless but unremovable.

"Anything else to declare?"

"I have a pair of Earth-made binoculars, a Terran camera, and half a bottle of Vainwal *firi*," I told him.

"Let's see them."

He opened the cases, and I tensed. This was the moment I had been dreading.

I should have tried to bribe him. But that would have meant—if he happened to be honest—a fine and blacklisting. I couldn't risk that.

He glanced at the camera and binoculars. Terran lenses are a luxury item and usually highly taxed. "Ten *reis* duty," he said, and pushed the folds of clothing aside. "If the *firi* is less than ten ounces, there's no tax. What is this?"

I thought I'd bite through my tongue when his hand gripped it. It felt like a fist squeezing my heart. I said through a contracted throat, "Let it alone!"

"What in the—" he dragged it out. It was like a nail raking along a nerve. He started to unwrap the cloth. "Contraband weapon, huh? You—hell, it's a *sword*!"

I couldn't breathe. The blue crystals in the hilt winked up at me, and his hand gripping it was too vast an agony to be borne.

"It's a—an heirloom in my family."

He looked at me queerly. "Well, I'm not hurting it any. Just wanted to make sure it wasn't a contraband blaster, or something." He shoved the folds of silk around it again, and I remembered how to breathe. He picked up the half-empty bottle of the expensive Vainwal cordial and measured it with his eyes. "About seven ounces. Sign a statement that you're bringing it in for personal consumption and not for resale, and it's duty free."

I signed. He snapped the lock on the case, and I moved, with faltering steps, away from the customs barrier.

One hurdle past. And I'd managed to live through it—this time. I rejoined Marius and went to hail a skycar.

CHAPTER TWO

The Sky Harbor Hotel was tawdry and expensive, and I didn't much like the place; but I wasn't apt to run into other Comyn there, and that was the main thing. So they showed us up to two of the square cubicles which Terrans call rooms.

I've gotten used to them on Terra and Vainwal, and they didn't bother me. But as I fastened the doors, I turned to Marius in sudden dismay. "Zandru's hells, I'd forgotten! Does this bother you?"

I knew how doors, and walls, and locks, could affect a Darkovan. I'd known that terrible, suffocating claustrophobia all during my first years on Earth. More than anything else it sets Darkovan apart from Terran; Darkovan rooms had translucent walls, divided by thin panels or curtains or solid light barriers.

But Marius seemed quite at ease, sprawling idly on a piece of furniture so modernistic I couldn't tell whether it was a bed or a chair. I shrugged; I'd learned to tolerate claustrophobia, probably he had too.

I bathed, shaved, and wadded up, carelessly, most of the Terran clothing I'd worn on the starship. The things were comfortable, but I couldn't turn up in Comyn Council wearing them. I dressed in suede-leather breeches, low ankle-boots, and laced up the crimson jerkin deftly, making a little extra display of my one-handed skill because I was still too damned sensitive about it. The short cloak in the Alton colors concealed the hand that wasn't there. I felt as if I'd changed my skin.

Marius was roaming restlessly about the room. He still didn't feel familiar. I vaguely recognized his voice and manner, but there wasn't

13

that sense of closeness usual between telepaths in a Comyn family. I
wondered if he sensed it, too. Maybe it was the drugs.

I stretched out, shut my eyes and tried to doze, but even the quiet
bothered me after eight days in space, the thrumming of the drives
an omnipresent nuisance under the veils of drug. Finally I sat up and
hauled my smaller piece of luggage toward me.

"Do me a favor, Marius?"

"Sure."

"I'm still doped—can't concentrate. Can you open a matrix lock?"

"If it's a simple one."

It was; any non-telepath could have attuned his mind to the simple
psychokinetic pattern broadcast by the matrix crystal which held the
lock shut. "It's simple, but it's keyed to me. Touch my mind and I'll give
it to you."

The request was not an uncommon one, within a telepath family.
But the boy stared at me in something like panic. I looked back,
amazed, then relaxed and grinned. After all, Marius hardly knew me.
He'd been a small boy when I left, and I supposed, to him, I was the
next thing to a complete stranger. "Oh, all right. Lock, and I'll touch
you."

I made a light telepathic contact with the surface of his thoughts,
visualizing the pattern of the matrix lock. His mind was so totally barriered that he might have been a stranger, even a non-telepath. It embarrassed me; I felt naked and intrusive.

After all, I wasn't sure Marius was a telepath. Children don't show
that talent to any extent before adolescence, and he'd been a child when
I went away. In all else he had inherited Terran traits, why should he
have this one Darkovan talent?

He laid the case, opened, on the bed. I lifted out a small square box
and handed it to him.

"Not much of a present," I said, "but at least I remembered."

He opened the box, hesitantly, and looked at the binoculars that lay, shiny and alien, inside. But he handled them with a strange embarrassment, then laid them back in the box without comment. I felt mildly annoyed. I hadn't expected gratitude, especially, but he might have thanked me. He hadn't asked about father, either.

"The Terrans can't be beaten for lensed goods," he said, after a minute.

"They can grind lenses. And build spaceships. As far as I can tell, it's all they can do."

"And fight wars," he said, but I didn't take that up.

"I'll show you the camera, too. I won't tell you what I paid for it, though—you'd think I was crazy."

I went through the cases, and Marius sat beside me, looking at things and asking diffident questions. He was obviously interested, but for some reason he seemed to be trying to conceal it. Why?

At last I drew out the long shape of the sword. And as I touched it, I felt the familiar mixture of revulsion and pleasure....

All the time I'd been off Darkover, it had been dead. Dormant. Hidden between blade and hilt of the heirloom sword, the proximity of the strong matrix made me tremble. Off-world it was an inert crystal. Now it was *alive*, with a strange, living warmth.

Most matrices are harmless. Bits of metal, or crystal, or stone, which respond to the psychokinetic wavelengths of thought, transforming them into energy. In the ordinary matrix mechanic—and in spite of what the Terrans think, matrix mechanics is just a science, which anybody can learn—this psychokinetic ability is developed independent of telepathy. Though telepaths are better at it, especially on the higher levels.

But the Sharra matrix was keyed into the telepathic centers, and into the whole nervous system, body and brain.

It was dangerous to handle. Matrices of this kind were traditionally concealed in a weapon of some sort. Sharra's matrix was the most fearful weapon ever devised. It was reasonable to hide it in a sword. A lithi-um bomb would have been better. *Preferably one that would explode and destroy matrix and all ... and me with it.*

Marius was gazing down at me, with a set, horror-stricken face. He was shaking.

"Sharra's matrix!" he whispered between stiff lips. "Why, Lew? Why?"

I turned on him, and demanded hoarsely, "How do you know—"

He had never been told. Our father had agreed to keep it from him. I got up, suspicion surging over me, but before I could complete the question, a burp from the intercom interrupted. Marius reached past me to grab it; listened, then held out the receiver and vacated his seat for me. "Official, Lew," he said in an undertone.

"Department three," said a crisp, bored voice, when I identified my-self.

"Zandru!" I muttered. "Already? No—excuse me—go ahead."

"Official notification," said the bored voice. "A statement of in-tention to murder, in fair fight, has been filed with this office against Lewis Alton-Kennard-Montray-Alton. Declared murderer is identified as Robert Raymon Kadarin, address unregistered. Notification has been legally given; kindly accept and acknowledge the notice, or file a legally acceptable reason for refusal."

I swallowed hard. "Acknowledged," I said at last, and put down the receiver, sweating. The boy came and sat beside me. "What's wrong, Lew?"

My head hurt, and I rubbed it with my good hand.

"I just got an intent-to-murder."

"Hell," said Marius, "already? Who from?"

"Nobody you know." My scar twitched. Kadarin—leader of the rebels of Sharra; once my friend, now my sworn, implacable foe. He hadn't lost any time in inviting me to settle our old quarrel. I wondered if he even knew I'd lost my hand. Tardily it occurred to me—as if it were something happening to someone else—that this would have been a legally admissible reason for refusing. I tried to reassure the staring boy.

"Take it easy, Marius. I'm not afraid of Kadarin, in fair fight. He never was any good with a sword. He—"

"Kadarin!" he stammered. "But, but Bob promised—"

"*Bob!*" Abruptly my fingers bit his arm. "How do *you* know Kadarin?"

"I want to explain, Lew. I'm not—"

"You'll do a lot of explaining, brother," I said curtly. And then someone started to hammer purposefully on the door.

"Don't open it!" said Marius urgently.

But I crossed the room and threw back the bolt, and Dio Ridenow ran into the room.

Since I'd seen her on the spaceport she had changed into men's riding clothes, a little too big for her, and she looked like a belligerent child. She stopped, a step or two inside, and stood staring at the boy behind me.

"What—"

"You know my brother," I said impatiently.

But Dio stood frozen. "Your *brother*?" she gasped, at last, "Are you out of your mind? That's no more Marius than—than I am!" I drew back incredulously, and Dio stamped her foot in annoyance. "His eyes! Lew, you idiot, *look at his eyes!*"

My supposed brother made a quick lunge, taking me off balance. He threw his whole weight against us. Dio reeled, and I went down on one knee, fighting for balance. *Eyes.* Marius—now I remembered—had had the eyes of our Terran mother. Dark brown. No Darkovan has brown or black eyes. And this—this impostor who was *not* Marius looked at me with eyes of a stranger, gold-flecked amber. Only twice had I seen eyes like that. Marjorie. And—

"Rafe Scott!"

Marjorie's brother! No wonder he had known me, no wonder I had sensed his presence as familiar. I remembered him, too, only as a small boy!

He tried to push past me; I grabbed at him and we swayed, struggling, in a bone-breaking clinch. *"Where's my brother?"* I yelled. I twisted my foot behind his ankle, and we crashed to the floor together.

He'd never said he was Marius, it flashed across my mind in a split second. *He just hadn't denied it when I thought so....*

I got my knee across his chest and held him pinned down. "What's the idea, Rafe? Talk!"

"Let me up, damn you! I can explain!"

I didn't doubt that a bit. How cleverly he had discovered that I was unarmed. But I should have known. I should have trusted my instinct; he didn't *feel* like my brother. He hadn't asked about father. He'd been embarrassed when I brought him a gift.

Dio said, "Lew, perhaps—" but before I could answer, Rafe gave an unexpected twist and sent me sprawling. Before I could scramble up, he thrust Dio unceremoniously aside, and the door slammed behind him.

I got up, my breath coming hard, and Dio came to me. "Are you hurt? Aren't you going to try and catch him?"

"No, to both questions." Until I found out why Rafe had tried this clumsy and daring imposture, there would be no point in finding him. And meanwhile, where was Marius?

"The situation," I remarked, not necessarily to Dio, "gets crazier every minute. Where do *you* come into it?"

She sat down on the bed and glared at me.

"Where do you think?"

For once I regretted that I could not read her mind. There was a reason why I couldn't—but I won't go into that now. But Dio was trouble, in a pretty, small, blonde package. I was here on Darkover; I had to stay at least a while.

The social codes of Vainwal—where Dio, under the lax protection of her brother Lerrys, had spent the last two seasons—are considerably less rigid than the strict codes of Darkovan propriety. Her brother had had sense enough not to interfere.

But here on Darkover, Dio was *comynara*, and held *laran* rights in the vast Ridenow estates. And what was I? A half-caste of the hated Terrans—entanglement with Dio would bring all the Ridenow down on my head, and there were a lot of them.

I would be grateful to Dio all my life. When Marjorie was torn from me, in the horror of that last night when Sharra had ravened in the hills across the river, something had been cut from me. Not clean like my hand, but rotting and festering inside. There had been no other women, no other love, nothing but a bleak black horror, until Dio. She had flung herself into my life, a pretty, passionate, willful girl, and she had gone unflinching into that horror, and somehow, after that, I had healed clean.

Love? Not as I knew the word. But understanding, and implicit trust. I would have trusted her with my reputation, my fortune, my sanity—my life.

But I trusted her brothers about as far as I could see through the hull of the *Southern Cross*. And I couldn't quarrel with them—not yet. I tried to make this clear to Dio without hurting her feelings, but it wasn't easy. She sat sulking and swinging her feet while I paced up and down like a trapped animal. Just having her here in my rooms could be dangerous if her family got wind of it—however innocent. And I knew if we were together very much it wouldn't be innocent. Dio's murmured "I understand," made me angry because I knew she did not really understand at all.

Her restless glance fell on the camouflage sword, lying across the bed. She frowned and picked it up.

Not pain, exactly, but a tension gripping me, a fist squeezing my nerves. I cried out, wordlessly, and Dio dropped it as if it burned her, staring open-mouthed.

"What's the matter?"

"I—can't explain." I stood regarding the thing for some minutes. "Before anything else, I'd better fix it so it's safe to handle. For the one who handles it and for me."

I rummaged my luggage for my matrix technician's kit. I had only a few lengths left of the special insulating cloth, but now I was back on Darkover, I could have more made for me. I wrapped the stuff around and over the juncture of hilt and blade until I could no longer feel the warmth and tingle of the matrix; frowned and held it away. I wasn't even sure if ordinary safeguards would work with this matrix.

I handed it to Dio. She bit her lip, but took it. It hurt, but manageably; a small nagging tension, no more. That much I could stand.

"Why ever did you leave a high-level matrix uninsulated?" Dio demanded, "and why did you let yourself be keyed into it that way?"

It was a very good question, especially the last. But I ignored that one. "I didn't dare bring it through customs under insulation," I said soberly. "Earthmen know, now, what to look for. As long as it was just a sword, no one would look twice at it."

"Lew, I don't understand," she said helplessly.

"Don't try, darling," I said. "The less you know, the better for you. This isn't Vainwal, and I'm—not the man you knew there."

Her soft mouth was trembling, and in another minute I would have taken her in my arms; but at that moment someone banged on the door again.

And I had thought I'd have privacy here!

I stepped away from Dio. "That's probably your brothers," I said bitterly, "and I'll have another intent-to-murder filed on me."

I stepped toward the door. She caught my arm. "Wait," she said, urgently. "Take this."

I stared without comprehension at the thing she held out to me. It was a small propulsion pistol: one of the Terran-made powder weapons which do unbelievable havoc for their size and simplicity. I drew back my hand in refusal, but Dio thrust it into my pocket. "You don't have to use it," she said, "just carry it. *Please*, Lew."

The knock on the door was repeated, but Dio held me, saying, "*Please*," again, until at last, impatiently, I nodded. I went and opened the door a crack, standing in the opening so the girl could not be seen.

The boy in the hallway was stocky and dark, with heavy sullen features and amused dark eyes. He said, "Well, Lew?"

And then the presence of him was tangible to me. I can't explain exactly how, but I *knew*. All at once it was unbelievable that Rafe could have fooled me for a minute. Proof, if needed, that I'd been operating at minus capacity when I landed. I said huskily, "Marius," and drew him inside.

He didn't say much, but his awkward grip of my hand was hard and intense. "Lew—father?"

"On Vainwal," I said. "There is a law. It is forbidden to transport bodies in space."

He swallowed and bent his head. "Under a sun I've never seen—" he whispered. I put my good arm round him, and after a minute he said thickly, "At least you're here. You did come. They told me you wouldn't."

Touched, a little ashamed, I let him go. It had taken a command to bring me back, and I wasn't proud of that, now. I looked around, but Dio had gone. Evidently she had slipped out of the room by the other door. I was relieved; it saved explanations.

But in a way I was annoyed, too. Entirely too many people had been turning up and vanishing again. All the wrong people, for all the wrong reasons. Dyan Ardais—picking my mind on the skyliner. The girl on the spaceport, who looked like Linnell and wasn't. Rafe, passing himself off as my brother when he wasn't. Dio, turning up for no good reason, and disappearing again. And now Marius himself had turned up! Coincidence? Maybe, but confusing.

"Are you ready to leave?" Marius asked. "I've made all the arrangements, unless you've some reason for staying here."

"I've got to pick up my matrix certification at the Legation," I said. "Then we'll go." Maybe the sooner I got out of here, the better—or half of Darkover would be bursting in on me playing games!

"Lew," Marius asked abruptly, "do you have a gun?"

Rafe's question—and it grated on me. I was readjusting my thoughts, taking the fake Marius—Rafe—out of my thoughts and putting my brother where he belonged in them.

I said curtly, "Yes," and let it go at that. "Will you come to the Legation with me?"

"I'll walk across the city with you." He looked around the closed-in room and shuddered. "I couldn't stay in this beast-pit. You weren't going to sleep here tonight, were you?"

THE TRADE CITY HAD grown during my absence; it was larger than I remembered, dirtier, more crowded. Already it seemed more natural to call it the Trade City than by its Darkovan name, Thendara. Marius walked at my side, silent At last he asked "Lew, what's it like on Terra?"

He would ask that. Earth, home of the unknown forefathers he resembled so much. I had resented my Terran blood. Did he?

"It would take a lifetime to know Terra. I was only there for three years. I learned a lot of science and a little mathematics. Their technical schools are good. There was too much machinery, too much noise. I lived in the mountains; trying to live at sea level made me ill."

"You didn't like it there?"

"It was all right. They even fixed up a mechanical hand for me." I made a grim face. "There's the Legation."

Marius said, "You'd better give me that gun," then stared, in consternation, as I turned on him. "What's the matter, Lew?"

"Something very funny is going on," I said, "and I am getting suspicious of people who want me unarmed. Even you. Do you know a man called Robert Kadarin?"

When Marius looked blank, that dark face could be a masterpiece of obscurity, as unrevealing as a pudding. "I think I've heard the name. Why?"

"He filed an intent-to-murder on me," I said, and briefly drew the pistol out of my pocket. "I won't use this. Not on him. But I'm going to carry it."

"You'd better let me—" Marius stopped and shrugged. "I see. Forget I asked."

I rode the lift upward in the HQ building, past the barracks of Spaceforce, the census bureau, the vast floors of machines, records, traffic, all the business of the Empire. I walked down the corridors of the top floor, to a door that said: DAN LAWTON—Legate of Darkovan Affairs.

I'd met Lawton briefly before I left Darkover. His story was a little like mine: a Terran father, a mother from the Comyn. We were remotely related—I'd never figured out how. He was a big, rangy redhead who looked Darkovan and could have claimed a place in Comyn Council if he'd wanted it. He hadn't. He'd chosen the Empire, and was one of the top-ranking liaison men between Terran and Darkovan. No man can be honest who lives by Terra's codes; but he came closer than most.

We shook hands in the Terran fashion—a custom I hated—and I sat down. His smile was friendly, not over-hearty, and he didn't evade my eyes—and there are not many men who can, or will, look a telepath square in the eyes.

He shoved the plastic chip across the table. "Here. I didn't need this; I just wanted a good excuse to talk to you, Alton."

I pocketed the certification, but I didn't answer.

"You've been on Terra, I hear. Like it?"

"The planet, yes. The people—no offense—no."

He laughed. "Don't apologize. I left, too. Only the dregs stay there. Anyone with any enterprise or intelligence goes out into the Empire. Alton, why did you never apply for Empire citizenship? Your mother was Terran—you had everything to gain by it, and nothing to lose."

"Why did you never accept a seat among the Hasturs?" I countered.

He nodded. "I see."

"Lawton, I don't fight Terra. I don't much like having the Empire here, but Darkover just doesn't fight by cities and nations and planets. If an Earthman were my enemy, I'd file an intent-to-murder, and kill him. If a dozen of them burned my house or stole my stud animals, I'd get my *com'ii* together and we'd kill *them*. But I can't feel anything at all about a few thousand people who have never done me either good or ill, just because they're *here*. It isn't our way. We do our hating by ones, not by millions."

"I can admire that psychology, but it puts you at a disadvantage against the Empire," Lawton said, and sighed. "Well, I won't keep you—unless there's something else I can do for you?"

"Maybe there is. Do you know a man who uses the name of Kadarin?"

The reaction was immediate. "Don't tell me he's in Thendara!"

"You know him?"

"I wish I didn't! No, I don't know him personally, I've never actually set eyes on him. But he pops up everywhere. He claims Darkovan citizenship when he's in the Terran Zone, and somehow manages to prove it; and I understand he claims to be a Terran, and prove it, outside."

"And?"

"And we can't deny him his Thirteen Days."

I chuckled. I had seen Terrans on Darkover baffled, before this, by the seemingly illogical catch-as-catch-can of the Thirteen Days. An exile, an outlaw, even a murderer, had an inalienable right—dating from time out of mind—to spend one day in Thendara, thirteen times a year, for the purpose of exercising his legal rights. During that time, provided he commits no overt offense, he enjoys absolute legal immunity.

"If he stayed one second over his limit, we'd grab him. But he's careful. We aren't even able to hold him for spitting on the sidewalk. The only place he ever goes is the Spacemen's Orphanage. After which, seemingly, he vanishes into thin air."

"Well, you may be rid of him soon," I said. "Don't prosecute me when I kill him. He's filed intent-to-murder on me."

"If I could only be sure it wouldn't work the other way," Lawton smiled, as I rose to go.

But as I crossed the threshold, he called me abruptly back. The friendliness was gone; he strode toward me, wrathfully.

"You're carrying contraband. Hand it over!"

I handed the gun to him. There must, of course, have been a clarifier screen there. Lawton clicked the chambers; then he stared, frowned and handed it back to me.

"Here. Take it. I didn't realize."

He thrust it at me, impatiently. "Go on, take it! But get out of here before anyone else catches you. And give it back. If you need a permit, I'll try to get you one. But don't go around carrying contraband!" He pushed the gun back into my hand and virtually shoved me out of the office. I turned it over, baffled, as I walked toward the elevator. Then my name fell on a small name plate: RAFAEL SCOTT.

And suddenly I knew I was not going to ask either Dio or Marius for an explanation.

CHAPTER THREE

"Very well, my lords. I will do as you wish!"

The woman's voice stopped me, cold, as I parted the curtains and stepped into the enclosure of the Altons, in the Council Hall of the Comyn.

We had come late to the Hidden City; so late that there had been no time to send word to Old Hastur or even to make my presence known to Linnell who, as my nearest kinswoman and foster sister, would have been informed at once. Marius, who had never been accepted in Comyn Council, had parted from me outside the council hall and gone to take his place in the lower hall among the lesser nobles and younger sons. I had climbed the stairs to the long gallery, intending to slip quietly through the curtains into the enclosure assigned to the Altons of the Comyn hierarchy.

I stood there, startled; for it was Callina Aillard who was speaking.

I had known her all my life, of course. She was my cousin, too: Linnell's half sister. But when I saw her last, six years ago—I shied away from the memory—she had been a girl, quiet, colorless. Now I saw that she was a woman, and beautiful.

She was standing, her head flung back, before the High Seat; a slender woman with fair fragile features in a dark robe. Gems were braided into her long hair; gold chains wound about her slender throat and a golden chain about her waist, giving her somehow the look of a prisoner, hung with fetters and yet defiant. Her voice rang out again, clear and angry.

"When before this has a Keeper been subject to the whims of the Council?"

So that was it!

Marius hadn't told me there was a new Keeper in Comyn Council, and I hadn't thought to ask.

In fact, he hadn't told me much. I looked down now, slipping into my seat behind the railings, at the Council Hall of the Comyn.

It was a high, vaulted room, filled with shadows and sunlight. In the lower hall, the lesser nobles were ranged; along the dais, or gallery, were the Comyn, each family in its own enclosure, ranged in a semicircle. In the center, in the High Seat, old Danvan of Hastur, Regent of the Comyn, was standing; behind him, in the shadows, was a young man I could not see clearly. Beside him, I recognized young Derik Elhalyn, Lord of the Comyn—ruling under Hastur until he reached his majority next year. Derik, lounging in a chair, looked bored.

I looked around, getting my bearings quickly. Dyan Ardais glanced up, with an enigmatic grin, as if he sensed my presence. Beyond him Dio Ridenow was seated among her brothers; I saw my cousin Linnell, but from where she sat I knew she could not see me.

But my eyes came back to Callina. A Keeper!

Not for years had there been a Keeper seated in Comyn Council. Old Ashara had kept to her tower during my lifetime, during my father's lifetime. She must be unbelievably ancient now. During my childhood, for a short time, there had been a frail flame-haired girl, veiled like a shrouded star, before whom even the Hasturs showed reverence. But when I was still a boy she had died or gone into seclusion, and since that day no young girls had been trained in the secrets of the master-screens. A few sub-keepers and matrix mechanics—I was one, when I cared to take my place among them—kept the relays working. It was hard to realize that my cousin Callina was the Keeper, holding in her frail hands all the incredible power of Ashara.

Yet I knew her courage. The thought roused painful memories. I didn't want to remember how and when I had last seen Callina.

Old Hastur spoke sternly.

"My lady, times have changed. In these days—"

"In these days they have changed indeed," she said, throwing back her head with a little silvery ringing of jewels, "when we have slavery on Darkover, and a Keeper can be sold like a shaol in the market place! No, hear me out! I tell you, we would do better to hand over all our secrets now to the accursed Terrans than to ally with the renegades out of Aldaran!"

Her eyes searched and abruptly met mine in the shadows, and unexpectedly she raised her arm and pointed a slender finger at me.

"And there sits one who can prove what I say!"

But I was already on my feet. *Ally with Aldaran?* I heard my own voice, unbidden.

"You damned, incredible fools!"

Abrupt silence was followed by a sudden stir, a murmur of voices, and a growl; and in dismay I realized what I had done. I had jumped feet first into an affair I really knew nothing about. But the name Aldaran was enough. I looked straight at Old Hastur and defied him.

"Did I hear you say "ally with Aldaran"? With that renegade clan whose name stinks all over Darkover? The men who sold our world to the Terrans?" My voice cracked like a boy's.

Beside Hastur, young Derik Elhalyn rose to his feet. He made a sign to Hastur and spoke informally.

"Lew, you're forgetting yourself," he said. Then, leaning forward, the sunlight gleaming on his red-gold hair, he spoke to the whole council, with a charming smile.

"Look here! A Comyn Lord comes back to us, after six years, and we do nothing to welcome him, but let him creep in like a mouse coming to his hole! Welcome home, Lew Alton!"

I cut through the round of applause he was trying to start. "Never mind that," I said. "Lord Hastur—and you, my prince, consider this! Aldaran's men were Comyn, once, and held council voice here. Why were they exiled? Ask yourself that! Or has the old shame been turned into a bedtime tale for children? Who gave the Terrans a foothold on Darkover? Are we all mad here? Or did I hear someone say—*ally with Aldaran?*"

I turned here and there, searching the shadowed faces for a sign of comprehension anywhere. "Do we want the Terrans on our doorstep?"

Then, desperately, I made my last appeal. I raised the arm that ends in a pinned-down sleeve, and I knew my voice was shaking.

"Do we want Sharra?"

There was a short, ugly silence. Then they all began talking at once. They didn't want to hear about that. The voice of Dyan Ardais rose, clear and cheerful, over the rest.

"That's your hate speaking, Lew. Not your good sense. Friends, I think we can excuse Lew Alton for his words. He has reason for prejudice. But those days are gone; we must judge by today's facts, not yesterday's old grievances. Sit down, Lew. You've been away a long time. When you know more about this, maybe you'll change your mind. Listen to our side, anyway."

There was a general murmur of approval. Damn him! Damn him, anyway! Shaking, I sat down. He had hinted—no, he had said right out—that I was to be pitied; a cripple with an old grudge, coming back and trying to take up the old feud where I left off. By skillfully focusing their unspoken feelings, he had given them a good reason to disregard what I said.

But the Aldarans had been at the center of the Sharra rebellion! Didn't they even know that?

Or didn't they want to know? The Sharra rebellion had only been a symbol, a symptom—like all civil wars—of internal troubles. The Aldarans were not the only ones on Darkover who were lured by the Terran Empire. The Comyn stood out, almost alone, against the magnet-like attraction of that star-spanning federation.

And I was an easy scapegoat for both sides. The Comyn conservatives distrusted me because I was half Terran, and the anti-Comyn faction distrusted me because my father, Kennard Alton, had been the staunchest leader of the Comyn. And they both feared what I knew of Sharra. In their minds I was still part of that terror which had flooded the countryside with "leathered Terrans wearing blasters, instead of honest swords, and making the clean night rotten with the spew of their rockets. They had never forgotten or forgiven that. Why should they?

"Our grandfathers drove the Aldarans out of the Comyn," said Lerrys Ridenow, "but it's high time we forgot their superstitious nonsense."

From the shadows behind Old Hastur, a young and diffident voice spoke up. "Why not hear all of what Lew Alton has to say? He understands the *Terranan*; he's lived among them. And he's kin to Aldaran. Would he speak against his own kinsmen without good cause?"

"Let us, at least, discuss this among the Comyn!" Callina said, and finally Hastur nodded. He spoke the formula that dismissed the outsiders; there was some muttering among the men in the lower hall, but gradually they began to quiet down, to rise and depart by twos and threes.

My head was beginning to ache, as always in this hall. It was, of course, filled with the telepathic dampers which cut out mental interference—a necessary precaution when a large number of Comyn were gathered. One of them was located right over my head. They were supposed, by law, to be placed at random; but somehow they always turned up almost in the laps of the Altons. Each family of the Comyn had its own particular gift, or telepathic talent; in the Altons, it was the hyper-developed telepathic nerve which could force rapport, undesired, or paralyze the minds of men, and the Comyn had always been a little afraid of the Altons. The Gifts are mostly recessive now, bred out by generations of intermarriage with non-telepaths, but the tradition remained, and the Altons always ended up with telepathic dampers in their laps. The continuous disrhythmic waves—half sonics, half energons—were a low-keyed annoyance.

The boy beside Hastur, who had spoken up for me, came down the long gallery toward me. By now I had guessed who he was: the old regent's grandson, Regis Hastur. As he passed Callina Aillard, she rose and, to my surprise, followed him.

"What is going to happen now?" I asked.

"Nothing, I hope." Regis smiled at me in a friendly way. He was one of those throwbacks, still born at times into old Darkovan families, to the pure Comyn type; fair-skinned, with the dark red hair of most Comyn, and eyes of almost metallic colorlessness. He was slightly built, and, like Callina, looked fragile; but it was the perfect tensile frailness of a dagger. He said, "So you've been out into space and back. Welcome, Lew."

"It sounds like a welcome, doesn't it?" I said dryly. "What's this about Aldaran? I came in only a few seconds before Callina pointed me out."

Regis moved his head toward the empty seats in the lower hall. "Politics," he said. "*They* want the Aldaran seated among the Comyn."

Callina interrupted. "And Beltran of Aldaran has submitted a request. He has the insolence, the—the damned effrontery—to want to come into the Comyn by marriage! By marriage—to me!" She was white with rage.

I whistled in blank amazement. That *was* effrontery. Oh, yes, outsiders could marry into Comyn council. The man who marries a *comynara* holds all privileges of his consort. But the Keepers, those women trained to work among the master-screens, are bound by very ancient Darkovan custom to remain virgin while they hold their high office. The very offer was an insult; it should have meant bloody death for the man who spoke it. Wars have been fought on Darkover for a good deal less than that. And here they were calmly discussing it in council!

Regis gave me an ironical glance. "As my grandfather said, times have changed. The Comyn aren't anxious to have a Keeper in council again."

I thought about that. Thirty-four years without Ashara would not make the council very eager to slip back under a woman's hand.

Looking at the whole thing objectively, it made sense. As Hastur said, times had changed. Whether we liked it or not, they changed. The office of Keeper had once been a dangerous and sacred thing. Once, or so my father told me, all the technology of Darkover had been done through the matrix screens, operated by the linked minds of the Keepers. All the mining, all the travel, all energy-requiring transitions—even nuclear dispersions—had been done through the energon rings, each linked in mind with one of these young girls.

But changes in technology had made it unnecessary. There was no need for the Keepers to give up all human contact and live behind walls, guarding their powers in seclusion. Conversely, there was no need for them to be deferred to, near-worshipped.

Callina smiled wryly, guessing my thoughts. "That's true," she said, "and I'm not greedy for power. But," she met my eyes steadily, "you know why I'm against this alliance, Lew. I don't want to bring it out in council, because it's your affair really. I don't like to ask you this, but I must. Will you tell them about Sharra and the Aldarans?"

I bowed over her hand, unable to speak.

For the sake of my sanity, I tried never to think or to speak about what the Aldarans, and their horde of rebels, had done to me—or to Marjorie.

But now I must. I owed Callina a debt I could never pay. At the awful end, when I had fled with Marjorie—both of us wounded, and Marjorie dying—it had been Callina who opened the Hidden City to us. That night, when the swords of Darkover and the blasters of the Terrans had hounded us, alike, Callina had dared exposure to the radioactive site of the ancient starships, and risked a terrible death herself, to give Marjorie a bare chance of life. It had been too late for Marjorie; but I could never forget.

Just the same—to drag it all out before the Council again—I felt the sweat break out on my forehead.

Regis said quietly, "You're the only chance we have, Lew. They might listen to you."

I swallowed. At last I said, "I'll—try."

"Try to do what? Stay sober long enough to welcome us all?" Derik Elhalyn thrust his way gaily between Regis and Callina, and gripped my shoulders. "Lew, old fellow, I didn't know you were on Darkover at all, until you popped up like one of those toys your father used to make for us! Dyan said it, but I'll say it again—welcome home!" He stood back, waiting for me to return the clasp, then his eyes fell on my empty sleeve. He said quickly, trying to cover up the awkward moment, "I'm glad you're back. We had some good times once."

I nodded, upset by his confusion, but glad of a pleasanter memory. "And will have more, I hope. Are the Elhalyn hawks still the finest in the mountains? Do you still climb the cliffs to take your own nestlings?"

"Yes, though I've not so much time now," Derik laughed. "Do you remember the day we climbed the north face of Nevarsin, hanging on by our eyebrows?" Once again he cut himself short, all too obviously remembering that I, at least, would never climb again. For my part, I was wondering what would happen to the Comyn when this scatterbrained lad assumed the place rightfully his. Old Hastur was a statesman and a diplomat. But Derik? For once I was glad of the telepathic dampers which kept them from following my thoughts.

Derik moved me toward the high seat, a hand on my shoulder. He said, "It was all arranged before your father died, you remember. But

Linnell's refused even to talk about setting a day for the marriage, until you were home again! So I have two reasons for welcoming you back!"

I returned his affectionate grin. I wasn't wholly alone, after all. I had kinsmen, friends. That marriage had been in the air since Linnell put away her dolls, yet it waited for my consent. "I haven't even seen Linnell yet," I said. "Though I thought I had."

I wondered if Linnell knew she had a double in the Terran Zone. I'd have to tell her that; it would amuse her.

But Hastur was calling us all to order again, and I took a seat between Regis and Derik. I was shocked at the small number of those who could claim blood-right in the Comyn; counting men and women alike, there were not three dozen. Yet they looked like a hostile army when, at Hastur's signal, I rose to face them.

I began slowly, knowing I must plead my cause without heat.

"If I understand this, you want to ally with Aldaran, to restore the old Seventh Domain to the Comyn. You're counting on this alliance to make peace with his mountain lords, and choke off all the outbreaks of rioting and war on the border. To get the co-operation of the Aldarans, in keeping the outlaws and renegades and Trailmen where they belong—on the other side of the Kadarin River. Maybe, even, to get us some Terran trade, and permits for machinery and planes, without making too many concessions to the Terrans themselves."

Lerrys Ridenow rose. "So far, you have been correctly informed," he drawled. "Can you tell us something new?"

"No." I turned, studying him. He was the only one of Dio's brothers worth the name of man, even when the term was used loosely. I'd known them, all three, on the pleasure moon off Vainwal. They were all delicate, effeminate, cat-graceful—and dangerous as so many tigers. They all tried to take the best of both worlds, a privilege which their great wealth, and the Comyn immunity from ordinary Darkovan laws, gave them. But Lerrys seemed to have the stuff of a man behind the languid, almost feminine mask, and he deserved an answer.

"No, but I can tell you something old. It won't work," I said. "Beltran of Aldaran, himself, is a decent sort of fellow. But he's tied himself up so tight with renegades and rebels and Trailmen and half-breed spies, he couldn't make peace with us if he wanted to. And you want to bring him into the Comyn?" I spread my hands. "Certainly. Bring in Beltran of Aldaran. Bring in the man they call Kadarin, and Lawton from Thendara, and the Terran Coordinator from Port Chicago, while you're about it!"

Hastur frowned. "Who is this Kadarin?" he asked.

"Hell, I don't know. Supposed to be kin to Aldaran."

"Like you," Dyan murmured.

"Yes. Half Terran, maybe. Rabble-rouser on any world that will hold him. They deported him from at least two other planets before he came back here. And that man Beltran of Aldaran, that man you want to marry to a Keeper, made Castle Aldaran into a hidey-hole for all of Kadarin's damned ridge runners and renegades!"

"Kadarin isn't a man's name," Lerrys said.

"And I'm not so sure he's a man," I retorted. The hills around Aldaran—you know what used to live back in those hills—all sorts of things you couldn't really call human. He looks human enough until you see his eyes." I stopped, turned inward on horror. Abruptly, remembering where I was, the wheels of my mind began to go round again.

"The name Kadarin is just defiance," I said. "In the hills across the river Kadarin, any bastard is called a son of the Kadarin. They say he never knew who or what his father was. When the Terrans hauled him in for questioning, he gave his name as Kadarin. That's all."

"Then he's working against the Terrans, too," Lerrys said.

"Maybe, maybe not. But he's tied up with Sharra—"

"And so were you," Dyan Ardais said softly. "But here you are."

My chair crashed over backwards. "Yes, damn you! Why else would I put myself through all of this, if I didn't know what hell it is? You think the danger's all over? If I can show you where Sharra is still out of control—not ten miles from here—then will you call off this crazy alliance?"

Hastur looked troubled, motioning Dyan and Lerrys to silence. "Can you do that, Lew? You're an Alton, and a telepath. But you couldn't do anything like that alone. You'd need a mental focus—"

"He's counting on that," Dyan sneered. "It's a good safe bluff! He's the last living adult Alton!"

From the shadows a voice said, "Oh, no he isn't."

Marius got slowly to his feet, and I stared at my brother in amazement. I thought he had left with the others. Could he—or would he—dare that most fearful of the Comyn powers?

Dyan laughed aloud. "You? You—*Terran*!" The word was an insult as he spoke it.

I was not yet ready to crawl away beaten. "Shall we turn off the dampers—and prove it on *you*, Lord Ardais?"

That was a bluff. I hadn't the faintest idea whether Marius had the Alton Gift, or whether he would go down in a screaming frenzy when my mind ripped into his. But Dyan did not know either, and his face was white before he lowered his eyes.

"It's still a bluff," said Lerrys. "We all know that Sharra's matrix was destroyed. What bugbear is this you drag out to frighten us, Lew? We are not children, to shiver at shadows! Sharra? *That* for Sharra!" He snapped his fingers.

I flung caution to the winds. "Destroyed hell!" I raged, "It's in my rooms this minute!"

I heard the gasps that ran round the circle. "*You* have it?"

I nodded, slowly. They wouldn't call me a liar again.

But then I caught a glimpse of Dyan's mocking eyes.

And suddenly I realized I had not been clever at all.

CHAPTER FOUR

Marius leaned across his saddle as I laid the insulated sword across the pommel of my own.

"Going to unwrap it here?"

Around us the thin morning air was as expressionless as his face. Behind us the foothills rose; and I caught the thin pungent smell of slopes scorched by forest fire, drifting down from the Hellers. Farther back in the clearing, the other Comyn waited.

My barriers were down, and I could feel die impact of their emotions. Hostility, curiosity, disbelief, or contempt from the Ardais and Aillard and Ridenow men; interested sympathy, and disquiet from the Hasturs and, strangely, from Lerrys Ridenow.

I would have preferred to do this thing privately. The thought of a hostile audience unnerved me. Knowing that my brother's life depended on my own nerves and control didn't help, either. Suddenly, I shivered. If Marius died—and he very likely would—only these witnesses would stand between me and a charge of murder. We were gambling on something we couldn't possibly be sure about; and I was scared.

The Alton focus is not easy. Having both parties aware and willing doesn't make it easy, even for two mature telepaths; it just makes it possible.

What we intended was to link minds—not in ordinary telepathic contact, not even in the forced rapport which an Alton—or, sometimes, a Hastur—can impose on another mind. But complete, and *mutual* rapport; conscious and subconscious mind, telepathic and psychokinetic nerve systems, time-scanning and coordinating consciousness, energonic functions, so that in effect we would function as one hyper-developed brain in two bodies.

My father had done it with me—once, for about thirty seconds—with my full awareness that it would probably kill me. He had known it was the only thing that would prove to them that I was a true Alton. It had forced the Comyn to accept me. I had been trained for days and safeguarded by every bit of his skill. Marius was taking it on almost unprepared.

I seemed to be seeing my brother for the first time. The difference in our ages, his freakish face and alien eyes, had made him a stranger; the knowledge that he might die beneath my mind, a few minutes from now, made him seem somehow less real; shadowy, like someone in a long dream. I made my voice rough.

"Want to back down, Marius? There's still time."

He looked amused again. "Jealous? Want to keep the *laran* privilege all to yourself?" he asked softly. "Don't want any more Altons in the Comyn, huh?"

I put the question point blank. "*Do* you have the Alton Gift, Marius?"

He shrugged. "I haven't the least notion. I've never tried to find out. What with one thing and another, I was given to understand that it would be unwarrantable insolence on my part."

I felt cold. That sentence outlined my brother's life. I'd have to remember that. There was a chance that what I gave him would *not* be death, but full Comyn status as an Alton. If he thought it was worth the gamble, what right had I to deny him? My father had gambled with me, and won. I lowered my head, and started to strip the insulating cloth from the sword.

"Is it a real sword?" Derik Elhalyn asked, guiding his horse toward us.

I shook my head, giving the hilt a hard twist. It came off in my hand, and I removed the silk-wrapped thing inside. A familiar hand crushed down on my chest.

"No," I said, "the sword's camouflage. You can look at it."

I thrust the pieces, hilt and blade, at him, but he backed away convulsively.

I saw the men hide unkind grins. But it wasn't funny—that Derik, Lord of the Comyn, was a coward. Hastur took the pieces and fitted them neatly together.

"The platinum and sapphires in this thing would buy a good-sized city," he said, "But Lew's got the dangerous part."

I stripped the matrix, feeling the familiar live warmth between my hands. It was egg-shaped and not quite egg-sized, a hunk of dull metal laced with little ribbons of shinier metal and starred with a pattern of blue winking eyes. "The pattern of sapphires in the sword hilt—sensitized carbon—matches the pattern of the matrix. They've altered my nerve reactions some way, to respond to it—" I stopped, my throat dry. What idiocy of self-flagellation had made me bring the thing back to Darkover? I was walking back, on my own feet, into the corner of hell that Kadarin had opened for me.

"Just what are you going to do?" Derik asked.

I tried to put it into words, he'd understand. All over the Hellers, there are certain spots which are activated—magnetized, somehow, to respond to the—the vibrations that key in Sharra. They can be used to draw on the power of Sharra."

Nobody asked the question I feared. *What is Sharra?*

I would have had to say I didn't know. I knew what it could do, but I didn't know what it was. Folklore says a goddess turned demon. I didn't want to theorize about Sharra. I wanted to stay away from it.

And that was the one thing I couldn't do.

Hastur took pity on me. "Once a certain locus has been put into key with the Sharra matrix, and the Sharra forces—as was done, years ago—a residue of power remains, and that spot can be drawn on. Lew has kept the matrix all these years, hoping for a chance to find these spots, through the original activator, and de-activate them. Once all the activated sites are released, the matrix can be monitored and then destroyed. But even an Alton telepath can't do that sort of work without a focus. One body can't handle that kind of vibration alone."

"And I'm the focus, if I live that long," Marius said impatiently. "Can we get on with it?"

I gave him one quick look; then, without further preliminary, made contact with his mind.

There is no way to describe the first shock of rapport. The acceleration of a jet, the hurt of a punch in the solar plexus, the shock of diving headfirst into liquid oxygen, might approximate it if you could live through all three at once. I felt Marius physically slump in his saddle under the impact of it and felt every defense of his mind concentrated to blocking me away. The human mind wasn't built for this. Blind instinct locked his barriers against me; a normal mind would die under the thrust needed to shatter that kind of resistance.

It was just as bald as that. If he had inherited the Alton Gift, he wouldn't die. If he hadn't, it would kill him.

Inwardly I was concentrated on Marius, in agonized concentration, but outwardly every detail around us was cut sharp and clear on my senses, as if etched there in acid; the cold sweat running down my body, the pity in the old Regent's eyes, the faces of the men around us. I heard Lerrys moaning, "Stop them! Stop them! It's killing them both!"

There was an instant of agony so great I thought I would scream aloud, the tension of a bow drawn back—and back—and bent to the very point where it must snap, where even the snap and break of death would be relief unspeakable.

Regis Hastur moved like a thrown spear; he tore the sword hilt from Hastur's hands and forced the matching pattern of gleaming stones into Marius' clenched fists. I saw, and felt, the agony dissolve in my brother's face, then the web of focused thought spread, gleamed, and wove together. Marius' mind firmed, held, a tangible rock of strength, against my own.

Alton! Terran blood in his veins—but true Alton, and my brother!

My sigh of relief caught almost into a sob. There was no need of words, but I spoke anyhow. "All right, brother?"

"Fine," he said, and stared at the sword hilt in his hands. "How the hell did I get hold of this thing?"

I handed him the Sharra matrix. I tensed in the familiar, breathless anticipation of anguish as his hands closed around it; but there was nothing but the familiar sense of rapport. I let my breath go.

"That's that," I said. "Well, Hastur?"

He made a brief, grave bow to Marius; a formal sign of recognition. Then he said quietly, "You're in charge."

I looked around at the mounted men. "Some of the activated spots are near here," I said, "and the sooner we break them up, the sooner we're safe. But—" I paused. I'd been so intent on the horror that possessed me, I hadn't thought to ask for a larger escort of mounted men. Besides the Hasturs, Dyan, Derik and the Ridenow brothers, there were only a scant half dozen guardsmen.

I said, "Sometimes the Trailmen come this close to the Hidden City—"

"Not since the 'Narr Campaign," said Lerrys languidly. His unspoken thought was clear. *You and your friends of Sharra stirred them up against us. Then you cleared out, but we did the fighting!*

"Just the same—" I looked up at the thick branches. Was it safe to ride so far with so few? Some of the Trailmen, far in the Hellers, are peaceful arboreal humanoids, no more harmful than so many monkeys. But those who have overflowed from the country around Aldaran, where every sort of human and half-human gathered, are a mixed breed—and dangerous.

Finally I shrugged. "I'm not afraid if you're not."

Dyan jeered, "You and your brother made a boast, Alton. Are you afraid someone will ask you to fulfill it?"

Nothing, I knew, would have suited him better than for Marius to break under my mind, and die.

I raised my eyes at Marius in question. He nodded, and we rode into the shadow of the trees.

For hours we rode under hanging branches, my mind in acute subliminal concentration on the power spots we could sense through the live crystal. My body and mind were aching with uncomfortable awareness; I wasn't used to this kind of prolonged mental strain any more—and what was more, I hadn't been on a horse since I left Darkover. They talk about the power of mind over matter. It doesn't work that way. A sore backside is just as effective an inhibitor of concentration as anything I know about.

The red sun had begun to swing downward when I reined in beside Hastur. "Listen," I said, low, "we're being decoyed. I was fairly sure no one else on Darkover knew I had the matrix, but someone must. Someone's taking power from the activated spots and drawing us."

He regarded me gravely. "Is that all?"

"I don't—"

He beckoned to Regis; the boy rode up and said, "We're being followed, Lew. I thought so before; now I'm sure of it. I've been in trailman country before this."

I glanced up at the thick branches, meeting overhead. Above there, I knew, old tree-roads wound in an endless labyrinth; but in these latitudes, I believed, they had been long deserted.

"We're in no shape to meet an armed attack," the Regent said. He looked uneasily at Regis and Derik, and I followed his thought—my barriers were all down now.

The whole power of the Comyn is here. One attack, now, could wipe us out. Why did I let them all come, unguarded? And then, a thought he could not conceal. *Are these Altons leading us into a trap?*

I gave him a bleak smile. "I don't blame you," I said. "As it happens, I'm not. But if anyone were around who really knew how to handle the Sharra power—I don't really—I'd be just a pawn. I might do just that."

The Regent did not question me. He turned in his saddle. "We'll turn back here."

"What's the matter?" Corus Ridenow sneered. "Have the Altons turned coward?"

By unlucky chance Marius was riding next to him; he leaned over abruptly and his flat hand smacked across Corus' face. The Ridenow reared back, and his hand swept down and flicked the knife loose from his boot—

And in that instant it happened!

Corus stopped dead, as if turned to stone, knife still raised; then, horribly loud in the paralyzed silence, Marius screamed. I have never heard such agony from a human throat. The full strength of the source flooded us both. God or demon force, machine or elemental—it was Sharra, and it was hell and, hearing a second outraged shout of protest, I did not even realize that I, too, had cried out.

And in that moment wild yells rang around us, and on every side men dropped from the trees into the road. A hand seized my bridle—and I knew just who had led us into the trap.

The man in the road was tall and lean; a shock of pale hair stood awry over a weathered gaunt face and steel gray eyes that glared at mine; he looked older, more dangerous than I remembered him. *Kadarin!*

My horse reared, almost flinging me into the road. Around me yells coalesced into a brawling melee; the clash of iron, the stamping and neighing of panicked horses. Kadarin bellowed in the guttural jargon of the Trailmen, "Away from the Altons! I want them!"

He was jerking my horse's bridle this way and that maneuvering to keep the animal's body between us. I swung to one side, almost lying along the horse's back, and felt the crack of a bullet past my ear. I yelled

"Coward!" and jerked at the reins, wheeling the horse abruptly. The impact knocked him sprawling. He was up again in a second, but in that second I was clear of the saddle and my sword was out—for what that was worth.

At one time I had been a fine swordsman, and Kadarin had never learned to handle one. Terrans never do. He carried one and he used it when he had to; it was the only way, in the mountains.

But I had learned to fight when I had two hands and I was wearing only a light dress-sword. Idiot that I was! I'd smelled danger, the air had been rotten with it—and I hadn't even worn a serviceable weapon!

Marius was fighting at my back with one of the nonhuman Trailmen, a lean crouched thing in rags with a long evil knife. The pattern of his strokes beat through our linked minds, and I cut the contact roughly; I had enough trouble with one fight. My steel clashed against Kadarin's.

He'd improved. In a matter of seconds he had me off balance, unable to attack, able only to keep up, somehow, a hard defense. Yet there was a kind of pleasure in it, even though my breath came short and blood dripped down my face with the sweat; he was here, and this time there was no man—or woman—to pull us apart.

But a defensive fight is doomed to lose. My mind worked, fast and desperately. Kadarin had one weakness; his temper. He would go into a flaming rage, and for a few minutes, that keen judgment of his went, and he was a berserk animal. If I could make him lose his temper for half a second, his acquired skill at swordplay would go with it. It was a dirty way to fight. But I wasn't in any shape to be fastidious.

"Son of the River!" I shouted at him in the Cahuenga dialect, which has nuances of filth unsurpassed in any other language. "Sandalwearer! You can't hide behind your little sister's petticoats *this* time!"

There was no change in the fast, slashingly awkward—but deadly—sword strokes. I hadn't really hoped there would be.

But for half a second he dropped the barriers around his mind.

And then he was my prisoner.

His mind gripped in the unique, locked-on paralysis of an Alton Telepath. And his body rigid—paralyzed. I reached out, taking his sword from the stiff fingers. I lost consciousness of the battle round us. We might have been alone on the forest road, Kadarin and I—and my hate. In a minute I would kill him.

But I waited a second too long. I was exhausted already from the struggle with Marius; a flicker of faltering pressure, and Kadarin, alert, leaped free with a savage cry. He outweighed me by half; the impact knocked me full-length to the ground, and the next minute something crashed and struck my head and I plunged miles into darkness.

A million years later, Old Hastur's face swam out of nowhere into focus before my aching eyes. "Lie still, Lew. You've been shot. They're gone."

I struggled to raise myself; subsided to the hands that forced me gently back. Through a swollen eye I counted the faces that swung around me in the red, murky sunset. Very far away, I heard Lerrys' voice, harsh and muted, mourning, "Poor boy."

I was bruised and in pain, but there was a worse ache, a great gaping emptiness torn loose, that made me deathly alone.

They didn't have to tell me that Marius was dead.

CHAPTER FIVE

I had a concussion. Kadarin's second bullet had knocked loose a splinter of bone; and Marius' death had been a shattering shock to the cells of my brain. The neuronic and synaptic links so recently made had all been torn apart again when he died, and for days my life—and sanity—hung in the balance.

I remember only shattering light and cold and shock, jolting movement, the pungency of drugs. Without any apparent sense of transition, one day I opened my eyes and found myself in my old rooms in the Comyn Castle in Thendara, and Linnell Aillard was sitting beside me.

She was very like Callina, only taller, darker, somehow gentler, with a sweet and childish face—although she was not really much younger than I. I suppose she was pretty. Not that it mattered. In every man's life there are a few women who simply don't register on his libido. Linnell was never a woman to me; she was my cousin. I lay contentedly watching her for some minutes, until she sensed my look and smiled.

"I thought you'd know me this time. Head ache?"

It did. I felt awkwardly at the ache, discovered bandages. Linnell caught my hand gently away.

"How long have I been here?"

"Here in Thendara? Only two days. You've been conscious for days and days, though."

"And—Marius?"

Her eyes filled with tears. "He is buried at the Hidden City. The Regent gave him full Comyn honors, Lew."

I freed my hand gently from hers and lay for a long time staring at the pattern of light on the translucent walls. Finally I asked, "The council?"

"They rushed it through, before we came here to Thendara. The marriage ceremony will be on Festival Night."

Life went on, I was thinking. "Yours to Derik?"

"Oh, no." She smiled, shyly. "There's no hurry about *that*. Callina's, to Beltran of Aldaran."

I sat bolt upright, disregarding knifing pain. "Do you mean they're still going through with that alliance? You're joking, Linnell! Or is everyone mad?"

She shook her head, looking troubled. "I think that's why they rushed it through; they were afraid you'd recover, and try to block them. Derik and the Hasturs wanted to wait for you; the others overruled them."

I didn't doubt that a bit. There was nothing the Comyn wanted less than a capable Alton in council. I threw back the covers. "I want to see Callina!"

"I'll ask her to come to you; you needn't get up."

I vetoed that. These rooms had been assigned to the Altons, during council season, for generations; they were probably well-monitored with telepathic traps and dampers. The Comyn had never trusted the male adult Altons too much. I wanted to see Callina somewhere else.

Her servants told me where to find her. I swung back an innocent-looking panel of curtain, and a flood of searing light literally exploded in my face. Swearing, I flung my hands over my tormented eyes; the closed lids dripped red and yellow after-images, and—a surprised voice spoke my name. The lights died down and Callina's face swam into focus.

"I am sorry. Can you see now? I must protect myself, you know, when I work."

"Don't bother apologizing." A Keeper among the matrix screens is vulnerable in ways ordinary people know nothing about. "I should have had more sense than to come in like that."

She smiled and held the curtain aside for me to pass through. "Yes. They told me you were a matrix worker."

And as she let the curtain fall, I suddenly became conscious of the subtle *wrongness* in her beauty.

One can tell everything about a woman by the way she walks. The very step of a wanton is suggestive. Innocence proclaims itself in carefree romping. Callina was young and lovely; but she did not move like a beautiful woman. There was something both very young and very old about her movements, as if the gawkiest stage of adolescence and the staid dignity of great old age had met, with no intermediary stage in her.

She let the curtains close, and the sense of strangeness vanished. I looked around the patterned walls, feeling the soothing effect of the even, diffused sonics. I had had an old, small matrix laboratory in the old wing, but nothing like this.

There was the regular monitor system, flashing with tiny star-like glimmers, one for every licensed matrix on every level in this section of Darkover. There was a specially modulated telepathic damper which filtered out telepathic overtones without confusing or inhibiting ordinary thought. And there was an immense panel with a molten-glass shimmer whose uses I could only guess; it might have been one of the almost legendary psychokinetic transmitters. Curiously prosaic, an ordinary screwdriver and some glittering scraps of insulating cloth lay on a table.

She said, "You know, of course, that they got away with the Sharra matrix?"

"If I'd had the brains of a mule," I said violently, "I'd have tossed it into a converter somewhere on Terra, and been well rid of it—and Darkover well rid of it too!"

"That *would* have put things out of control, forever; at best, Sharra was only dormant while the matrix was off-world. Destroying the matrix would have ended any hope of putting the activated sites out of action. Sharra isn't on the master banks, you know. It's an illegal matrix—unmonitored. We can't monitor it until all the loose sites and the free energy are located and controlled. What was the pattern?"

I let her tune out the dampers, and tried to project the pattern on a monitor screen; but only blurs swirled against the crystal surface. She was contrite. "I shouldn't have let you try that so soon after a head injury! Come out of here and rest!"

In a smaller room, whose open sky-wall looked down into the valley, I relaxed in a soft chair, while Callina watched me, aloof and reflective. I asked finally, "Callina, if you knew the pattern, could you duplicate the matrix and monitor the focal sites with the duplicate?"

She didn't even have to think it over. "No. I can duplicate a first or second level matrix like this—" She touched the tiny crystals that held her blue dress together over her breast. "And I might be able to construct a matrix lattice of complexity equal to the Sharra one—although I wouldn't care to try it alone. But two identical matrices of fourth level or higher can't exist simultaneously, in one universe and in time, without space distortion."

"Cherillys' Law," I recalled. "A matrix is the only unique thing in spacetime, and thus existing without any equilibrium point, has the power to shift energy."

She nodded. "Any attempt to make an exact molecular duplicate of a matrix like the one commanding Sharra—is it ninth level or tenth?—would warp half the planet right out of spacetime."

"I was afraid of that," I said, "but I told myself only a Keeper would really know."

"Keeper!" She gave a short, wry little laugh.

At last she said, "Linnell told you, I suppose? Lew, it isn't just the alliance that bothers me. If they're determined to put me out of the way, make sure I won't seize council power—well, they will. I can't stand against them all, Lew. If they think the alliance will help the Comyn, who am I to argue? Hastur is no fool. They could be right. I don't know anything about politics. If I weren't a Keeper, they wouldn't even have asked my consent as a formality; they would say marry, and I would marry! I suppose one husband is as good as another," she said, and again I had the curious impression of extreme age and naive youth, superimposed on the beautiful woman who sat watching me. She spoke of her own marriage as a passive little girl, married by proxy to a doll, might speak. Yet she was a beautiful and desirable woman. It was uncanny!

"It's the rest of it," she went on after a minute. "I can't believe ordinary Trailmen would know enough to attack you, just then, and steal the Sharra matrix. Who set them on?"

I stared. "Didn't Hastur tell you who set them on?"

"I don't think he knew."

"Trailmen," I said with angry emphasis, "would steal weapons, food, clothing—jewelry, perhaps—they would never dare to touch a matrix! And *that* matrix—why am I still alive, then?" I demanded. "Callina, I was keyed *into* that thing, body and brain! Even when it was insulated, if any out-of-phase person so much as laid a hand on it, it *hurt*! There are three people on the planet who could handle it without killing me! Didn't they tell you it was Kadarin himself?"

Her face went white. "I don't think Hastur would know Kadarin by sight," she said. "But how did Kadarin know you had the matrix?"

I did not want to think Rafe Scott would have betrayed me to Kadarin. The fires of Sharra had singed him, too. I'd rather believe that Kadarin could still read my mind, even from a distance. Suddenly, my loss hit me with overwhelming pain. Now I was absolutely alone.

"Don't grieve," Callina said softly. But I knew; to her, Marius had been only an alien, a half-caste, despised for his difference. How could I explain to Callina? We had been in total rapport, Marius and I, for perhaps three hours, with all that implies. I had known Marius as I knew myself; his strengths and weaknesses, his desires and dreams, hopes and disappointments. Years of living together could have told me no more. Until the moment of rapport I had never known a brother and until his dying mind ripped from mine I had never known loneliness. But there was no way to explain this to her.

Finally she asked, "Lew, how did you first get yourself involved with—" She started to say, *with Sharra*, looked at my twisting face and didn't. "With Kadarin? I never knew."

"I don't want to talk about it," I said curtly. *Again and again—must those old wounds be torn?*

"I know it's not easy," she said. "It's not easy for me to be handed over to Aldaran." She did not look at me again. She took a cigarette from a crystal dish, and sparked it alight with the jewel in her ring. I reached for one and fumbled it; she raised her head and frankly stared, and I looked at her defiantly.

"Men smoke on some planets."

"I don't believe it!"

"They do." Still defiant, I took one, remembered I had no light, and reached clumsily for her hand, raising her ring to light it. "And no one laughs. Or considers them effeminate. It is an accepted custom which causes no curiosity. And I learned to like it. Do you think you can endure the sight, Callina *comynara?*" We looked at each other in a blaze of hostility which had nothing to do with the small and silly argument over the cigarette.

Her lip curled. "One would expect it of the *Terranan,*" she said scornfully. "Please yourself."

I was still holding her hand and the ring. I let them go, drawing in a deep breath of the thin sweetish smoke. "You asked me a question," I said, staring at the distant snow-capped peaks. "I'll try to answer.

"Kadarin was Aldaran's foster brother, I've heard. No one knows who, or what, his parents were. Some say he's the son of a Terran renegade, Zeb Scott, by one of the nonhuman *chieri,* back in the hills.

Whatever he is, or isn't, he has the mind of a clever man. He learned some matrix mechanics—don't ask me how. He worked a while in Terran intelligence, got deported from two or three worlds, finally settled in the Hellers. Some of the Terrans back there have Darkovan, even nonhuman blood. He started organizing the rebels, the malcontents. Then he found me."

I got up and walked away from her. "You know what my life had been. Here—a bastard, an alien. Among the Terrans—a telepath, a freak. Kadarin, at least, made me feel that I belonged somewhere."

Not even to myself did I want to admit that once I had liked the man. I sighed.

"I spoke about a renegade, Zeb Scott."

The flood of memory rushed on, resistless, only a few bald words escaping to fill in years of adventure and the long search. "Zeb Scott died drunk, raving, in a wineshop in Carthon, babbling about the blue sword with the power of a hundred demons. We guessed that it was Sharra.

"The Aldarans, centuries ago—so the legend ran—had summoned Sharra to this world; but the power had been sealed off again, and the Aldarans exiled for their crime. Only after that had the Aldarans played traitor to Darkover, and sold the Terrans a foothold on our world.

"Kadarin went after the Sharra sword, found it, and experimented with the power. He needed a telepath. I was right at hand, and too young, too damned reckless to know what I was doing. And there were the Scotts. Rafe was just a child then. But there were the girls: Thyra, and Marjorie—"

I quit there. It was no use. There was no way, no way at all to tell her about Marjorie. I flung my cigarette savagely from the window and watched it spinning away on a little eddy of wind.

Callina said softly, when I had almost forgotten her, "What was he trying to do?"

This was safe ground. "Why does any traitor steal or betray? The Terrans have been trying for centuries to beg, borrow or steal some secrets of matrix mechanics. The Comyn were incorruptible, but Kadarin knew the Terrans would pay well. Experimenting with the power, he activated some of the focal points, showed them what he could do. But at the end he betrayed the Terrans too, and opened up a—a hole in space, a Gate between worlds, to take on all that power—"

My voice cracked like a boy's. "Damn him! Damn him waking and sleeping, living and dead, here and hereafter!" I fought suddenly back to self-control and said quietly, "He got what he wanted. But Marjorie and I were at the poles of power, and—"

I shook my head. What more could I say? The monstrous terror that had flamed and ravened between worlds, the hellfire. Marjorie, confident and unafraid at the pole of power, suddenly crumpling in agony, under the backlash of that awful thing—

"I broke out of the matrix lock, and somehow managed to slam the Gate again. But Marjorie was already—"

I broke there, unable to say another word, and slumped into a chair, hiding my face on my arm. Callina came swiftly to me, kneeling, her arms around my bent shoulders. "I know, Lew. I know."

I jerked away from her touch. "You know! Thank your Gods you don't know!" I said savagely. Then, gripped in the fist of memory, I let my head fall forward on her breast. She did know. She had tried to save us both. Marjorie had died in her arms. "Yes," I muttered, "you know the rest."

My head was throbbing, and I could feel the echoing *throb-throb* of her heart through the soft silk of her dress. Her hair was like the dust of flowers against my face. I raised my good hand to clasp her soft fingers in mine.

She threw back her head and looked at me.

"We're alone with this, Lew. Hastur's bound by Compact to obey the council. Derik's an imbecile, and Regis is only a boy. The Ridenow, the Ardais—they want anything that will keep them in power; they'd sell out to Sharra themselves if they thought they could do it safely! You're powerless alone. And I—" her mouth worked, but no sound came.

Finally she said, "I'm a Keeper, and I could hold all the power of Ashara if I would. Ashara would give me strength enough to rule the whole council if I would let her, but I—I won't be a puppet, Lew, I don't want to be only her pawn! I won't! The council pulling me one way, Ashara the other. Beltran couldn't be worse!"

We were clinging together like children frightened by the darkness. She was soft in my arms. I tightened my clasp on her; then her half-breathed protest went lax in the middle of a kiss. She made no resistance when I lifted her to her feet and drew back her head beneath my own.

Outside the last red trace of the sun dropped behind Nevarsin Peak and the stars began to wink in the denuded sky.

CHAPTER SIX

At the height of Comyn power, centuries ago, the Crystal Chamber must have seemed small for all those who could claim blood-right in the hierarchy. An even blue light spilled diffused radiance over the glass walls; green, scarlet, golden flashes struck through. At noon it was like dwelling in a rainbow's heart; at night it seemed to hang high and alone, buffeted on the winds of space.

Here I had first been presented to the Comyn, a boy of five, too big-boned and dark for a true Comyn child; young as I had been I remembered the debates, and old Duvic Elhalyn shouting, "Kennard Alton, you waste our time and insult this holy place bringing your half-caste bastard into Council!"

And I could see in memory my father turning savagely to lift me high above them, in full sight of the Comyn. "Look at the boy, and eat those words!" And the old Lord had eaten them. No one ever defied my father twice. Much good his raging had done. Half-caste I was, bastard I remained, alien I was and would be; as much as that small boy who had sat for hours, fidgeting through the long ceremonials he did not understand, arm aching from the touch of the matrix that had set its pattern in the flesh to seal his Comyn. I glanced impassively at my wrist. I still had the mark. About three inches above where they had had to take off my hand.

"What are you brooding about?" Derik demanded.

"Sorry. Did you ask me something? I was thinking about my first council. There were more of us then."

Derik laughed. "Then it's high time you began raising sons to follow you, laggard!"

The thought was not unpleasant. My own estates, fertile green valleys in the uplands around Daillon, were waiting for me. I glanced at Callina; she sat beside Linnell, the two snuggled together in a great chair that would have held half a dozen girls their size. Derik went over to them and stood talking to Linnell. She looked happy, and the prince's shallow handsome face seemed lighted from within. Not really stupid, Derik; only dull.

Not good enough for Linnell. But she loved him.

Dio Ridenow caught my eyes, then lowered her own with a resentful flush. Dyan Ardais came through the prism door, and I frowned suspiciously. Dyan, and Dyan alone, had known I had the Sharra matrix. Marius, while I was away, had been nothing more than a lonely boy, despised by the Comyn for his alien blood, powerless. I, alone, was powerless and maimed. But together we formed a powerful threat to his ambition.

Kadarin's attempt on my life was a personal feud, and he had fairly filed his intentions. The Trailmen would always steal. But would they risk killing an Alton, even by accident? Reprisals for such things were swift and terrible—or had been when the Comyn was worthy of the name. With swift decision, I reached out and made contact with Dyan's mind. He scowled and raised his head, locking barriers against me; and I did not take up the challenge. Not yet.

Hastur was calling us to order. This was a formality, of course; a gesture toward appeasing those who had been absent or ill. Ostensibly, since this closing ceremony of Comyn could not be held unless everyone who held *laran* rights in the Comyn were present, no member could complain that he had no chance to be heard. In theory I could keep them there as long as I chose—I, or any dissatisfied member—simply by refusing my assent to close the session. But in fact, any triviality, and small time-consuming matter, would be brought up and argued at length; anything to keep me from getting a chance to speak. Until time, or weariness, brought the session to an end and silenced me on those issues forever. Once the council was closed, I was bound by Comyn law and many oaths to contest the issues no further. I'd seen the blocking technique used before.

The triviality was not long in coming. Lerrys Ridenow arose and glared belligerently around the room, and Hastur stretched his baton to Lerrys, ignoring me.

"Comyn, I have a personal complaint—"

I saw Dio's hands knot into small fists. Would Lerrys really drag that affair out in Comyn council, or demand satisfaction from me at this late date and on another planet? But Lerrys did not look at me, but at Derik.

"My lords, in these days when the Comyn and the other powers of Darkover drift apart, our young ruler should take a consort outside of council, and bring in some strong alliance. Linnell Aillard, too, could give marriage-right to some strong and loyal man."

I stared. Dio and I had escaped public censure—but this was almost as bad. Linnell was white with shock, and Callina broke in angrily, rising to her feet, "Linnell is my ward! This is no matter for council meddling!"

Dyan caught up the phrase maliciously. "Meddling? Does a Comyn Keeper question the will of the council?"

"Not where I am concerned," Callina retorted, standing straight and defiant. "But for Linnell, yes!"

I knew this was only a point of delay, but I could not look at Linnell's small stricken face and keep silent. "Idiots!" I said harshly. "Yes, you too, Lord Regent! You very cleverly rushed the council through while I was out of my head—"

"From his utter disregard of council manners," drawled Lerrys in languid rebuke, "Lew Alton is still out of his head."

"Then more of you should have your wits addled like that," I retorted, turning on him. "This council is a farce, and now it is turning into a brawl! Here we sit like gaffers in the market square, haggling over marriages! Can a burst dam be mended with toothpicks?"

They were all listening to me, but I stopped, a familiar fist squeezing my throat. *What was this?*

Callina's face seemed to waver in the rainbow shimmer—or was it my eyes? But she caught up my words.

"Oh, we are so safe, my lords, we have so much time for this nonsense! While the Terrans lure the people away, and make a reeking, filthy Trade City out of our Thendara, we sit wrangling among ourselves, letting our young lords and ladies enjoy themselves on other planets—" her glance rested coldly on Dio Ridenow—"while we sit in the Crystal Chamber making marriages. And Sharra's matrix in Kadarin's hands! You had a demonstration, the other day, of our Comyn powers and what did you do? You let Marius Alton be killed, and Lew hurt. Those two you should have guarded above all the others! Which of you can answer for the life of Marius? Which of you would dare take his place?"

Before anyone could answer, I jumped in again.

"The Terrans have left us a little power to rule, and we play with our corner of the planet like little children squabbling over their playgrounds! The people used to hate the Terrans! Now they hate us instead! A leader could jump up from anywhere, or nowhere, and strike fire to all this tinder! While I was on Earth, I heard someone call Darkover the weak link in the Terran Empire. We could be the link to snap the chain of conquest! Are we doing it?"

Abruptly I stopped, out of breath, aware, first, that Callina and I were in telepathic contact—in spite of the dampers—and, second, that even this faint surface contact was exhausting me completely. I sent a desperate command: *Break it! Get out!* What was the girl doing? I couldn't hold that kind of rapport under a damper! She clung, uncomprehending, and I lashed out, with a quick telepathic surge, to knock her out of rapport. I was already so limp I could hardly stand up. I caught at the edge of the railing and let myself slide back into my seat, but I could not loose the merciless grip on my mind. *Was* it Callina?

The room was very quiet. I saw Dio's face, taut and pale. Lerrys choked, "What's wrong with the dampers?"

Hastur stood up, leaning over the long table, and started to speak, then looked up. His mouth dropped open.

Callina froze, motionless.

The floor dipped under my feet and would not stay still. And above us there was a little shimmering, a distortion of the air.

Dio screamed.

"The—the death sign," someone faltered, and voices died in deadly silence.

I stared at the sign that flared like letters of living fire in the air, and I felt my blood freeze and the strength running out of me like water. Twisted space writhed and flared, and the inside me was howling and gibbering, reduced to primal panic. *From time out of mind, before Darkover's sun faded to a dying ember, that sign meant doom and death, bodies and minds seared to ruin.*

"Sorceress! She-devil!" It was Dyan's voice exploding in curses; he took three quick strides toward Callina, caught her by the shoulders and wrenched her away from her place before the High Seat; flung her, with all the strength in his lean body, out into the room.

And young Regis, through some uncanny sensing, leaped up and caught Callina's reeling body as she fell. The sight broke the static horror that held me; I whirled to face Dyan. At last I had reason! The man who dared to touch a Keeper had forfeited immunity. Annihilating fury swept from me, taking Dyan unaware. The Alton Gift, even unfocused, can be a vicious thing. His mind lay, in seconds, stripped before mine. I rained vicious mental slaps on it. It was immensely satisfying. I had been holding this in check ever since he picked my mind on the skyliner. He writhed, crumpled and fell, gasping in loud desperate hoarse half-sobs.

The pattern of fire flamed and died and was gone. Space in the room was quiet, normal again.

Callina stood leaning on Regis, pallid and shaken. I still stood over Dyan; his defenses were slashed away, and it would have been easy to snap the thread of his life. But Derik threw himself forward, flinging restraining arms around me.

"What are you about, you madman?"

There is something in a touch which can lay the mind bare. And what I touched then, shook my world. Derik was a weakling; I had always known that; but this—this tumbling, impassible confusion? I drew away, unable to endure even a second of it, letting my savage attack on Dyan relax.

Hastur's voice, harsh, and somber, commanded, "In the name of Aldones! Let us have peace here, at least!"

Dyan stumbled to his feet and backed away. I could not move, though I had no will left to defy Hastur. The Regent looked gravely at Callina.

"A serious occasion, Callina *comynara.*"

"Serious truly. But only for me?" She freed herself from Regis' protecting arm. "Oh, I see. You blame me for the—the manifestation?"

"Who else?" Dio cried shrilly. "So innocent, so innocent she looks, but she and Ashara—she and Ashara—"

Callina turned terrible eyes on her.

"Can all your life be told in open council then, Dio Ridenow *comynara?* You sought Ashara once."

Dio's eyes sought mine. Then, with the quick desperate move of one deserted, she threw herself into the arms of her brother Lerrys and burrowed her bright head in his shoulder.

Callina faced them all with aloof dignity. "I need not defend myself from your silly panic, Dio," she said. "But you, Dyan Ardais, I ask no courtesies of you, but you touch me again at your life's risk. Let everyone hear, and let him beware of a finger's weight laid on me; I am Keeper. *And no man lives to maul me three times.*"

She turned toward the door. And until the curtains had folded down softly behind her, there was silence.

Then Dyan laughed, low and ugly. "In six years you have not changed, Lew Alton. Still you have a passion for witches. You stand here defending our sorceress, even as you once threw away all your Comyn honor for that mountain hellion of Kadarin's, trying to lure a Comyn lord to her bed—"

But that was all he got to say. "Zandru's hells!" I shouted, "she was my wife and you keep your filthy tongue from her name!" I smashed my flat hand, hard, across that sneering mouth. He yelped and staggered back, then his hand swept like lightning into his shirt—

And Regis was on him like lightning, seizing the small deadly thing he raised to his lips. The boy flung it to the floor in disgust. "A poison-pipe—in the Crystal Chamber! And you spoke of honor, Dyan Ardais?"

The two Hasturs held Dyan back between them. One of the Ridenow brothers had a restraining hand on my arm, but he didn't need it.

I'd had all I could stand.

I turned my back on them all and left.

I'd have strangled if I'd stayed there another minute.

Not knowing or caring where my steps led, I went up and up toward the height of the Comyn Castle. I found bitter relief in climbing flight after flight of stairs; head bent and aching, but a need for physical action driving me on.

Why the hell hadn't I stayed on Terra?

That damnable sign! Half the Comyn would take it for a supernatural apparition, a warning of danger. It meant danger, all right, but there was nothing supernatural about it. It was pure mechanics, and it scared me more than any ghostly visitation.

It was a trap-matrix; one of the old, illegal ones, which worked directly on the mind and emotions, rousing racial memories, atavistic fears—all the horrors of the freed subconscious of the individual and the race, throwing man back to the primal, reasonless beast.

Who would build a pattern like that?

I could have, but I hadn't. Callina? No Keeper alive would blaspheme her office that way. Lerrys? He might think it a perverted joke, but I didn't think he had the training. Dyan? No, it had scared him. Dio, Regis, Derik? Now we were getting silly; I'd be accusing Old Hastur, or my little Linnell, next!

Dyan, now. I couldn't even have the relief of killing him in fair fight.

Even with one hand, I wasn't afraid to fight him. Not a man Dyan's age. I don't read my antagonist's mind, like a telepath in a bad scare-story, to figure out his sword strokes. That sort of stuff takes intent, motionless concentration. Nobody—not the legendary Son of Aldones—could fight a duel that way.

But now I could fight him before a hundred witnesses, and they'd still cry murder. After today and what they'd seen me do to Kadarin. I couldn't do that to anyone else; Kadarin and I had once been in rapport through Sharra, and we had—however little we liked it—a foothold in each other's minds.

But Dyan didn't know that.

Dyan didn't know this either, but he'd had his revenge already.

Six years of knocking around the Empire had cured me, as far as cure was possible. I am not, now, the shattered youngster who had fled Darkover years ago. I am not the young idealist who found, in Kadarin, a hope of reconciling his two warring selves, or saw in a girl with amber eyes everything he wanted in this world or the next.

Or I thought I wasn't. But the first knock on my shell had cracked it wide open. What now?

I was standing on a high balcony, jutting out over the walls of the Comyn Castle. Below, the land lay spread like a map, daubed in burnt sienna and red and dusty gold and ochre. Around me rose the iridescent castle walls, which gave back the dropping light of the red sun, setting in blood and fire. *The bloody sun.* That is what the Terrans call the sun of Darkover. A just name—for them, and for us.

And far above me soared the high spire of the Keeper's Tower, arrogantly, aloof from castle or city. I looked up at it, apprehensively. I did not think that Ashara, ancient though she must be, would remain aloof from a holocaust in the Comyn.

Someone spoke my name and I turned, seeing Regis Hastur in the archway.

"I've got a message for you," he said. "I'm not going to give it, though."

I smiled grimly. "Don't, then. What is it?"

"My grandfather sent me to call you back. As a matter of fact, I wanted an excuse to get out myself."

"I suppose I ought to thank you for pulling that blow-pipe away from Dyan. Right now, I'm inclined to think you'd have saved us all trouble if you'd let him use it."

"Are you going to fight him?"

"How can I? You know what they say about the Altons."

The youngster joined me at the railing. "Want me to fight him as your proxy? That's legal, too."

I tried to hide how much the offer had touched me. "Thanks. But you'd better keep out of this business."

"It's too late for that. I'm in it already. Waist-deep."

I asked, on impulse, "Did you know Marius well?"

"I wish, now, that I could say yes." His face held a queer sort of shame. "Unfortunately—no, I never did."

"Did anybody?"

"I don't think so. Although he and Lerrys were friends, in a way." Regis traced an idle pattern in the dust, with his boot heel. After a minute he rubbed his toe over it and said, "I spent a few days in the Ridenow *forst* before coming to council, and—" he paused. "This is difficult—I heard it by chance, and the only honorable thing I could do, was to pledge not to repeat it. But the boy is dead now, and I think you have a right to know."

I said nothing. I had no right to insist that a Hastur violate his word. I waited for him to decide. At last he said, "It was Lerrys who suggested the alliance with Aldaran, and Marius himself went to Castle Aldaran as ambassador. Do you think Beltran would have had the insolence to *offer* marriage to a Keeper, unsolicited?"

I should have realized that. Someone must have told Beltran that such an offer would meet with serious consideration. But was Regis breaking his pledge, just to tell me my brother had been pawn-hand in a mildly treasonable intrigue?

"Can't you *see?*" Regis demanded. "Why *Callina?* Why a Keeper? Why not Dio, or Linnell, or my sister Javanne, or any of the other *comynara?* Beltran wouldn't care. In fact he'd probably have an ordinary girl, provided she could give him *laran* rights in council. No. Listen, you know the law—that a Keeper must remain a virgin, or she loses her power to work in the screens?"

"That's nonsense," I said.

"Nonsense or not, they believe it. The point is, this marriage launches two ships on one track. Beltran allied to them and Callina out of the council's way by good, fair, safe, legal means."

"It begins to fit together," I said. "Dyan and all." There was, after all, something Dyan wanted less than a capable, adult male Alton in council; a Comyn Keeper might be even more of a threat to him. "But that marriage will take place only over my dead body."

He knew immediately what I meant. "Then marry her yourself, *now,* Lew! Do it illegally, if you have to, in the Terran Zone."

I grinned ironically and held out my mutilated arm. I could not marry, by Darkovan law, while Kadarin lived. An unsettled blood-feud takes precedence over every other human obligation. But by Terran law we could marry.

I shook my head, heavily. "She'd never consent."

"If only Marius had lived!" Regis said, and I was moved by the sincerity of his words; the first honest regret I had heard from anyone, though they had all expressed formal condolences. I liked it better that he did not pretend to any personal sorrow, but simply said, "The Comyn needed him so. Lew, could you use any other telepath—me, for instance—for a focus like that?"

"I don't know," I said. "I don't think so. I'd rather not try. You're a Hastur, and it probably wouldn't kill you, but it wouldn't be fun." My voice suddenly turned hard. "Now tell me what you really came here to tell me!"

"The death sign," he blurted, then his face crumpled in panic. "I didn't mean that, I didn't—"

I could have had his confidence if I had waited. Instead I did something that still shames me. I caught one of his wrists with my good hand, and with a quick twist, a trick hold I'd learned on Vialles, forced him against the railing. He started to leap at me, then I caught his thought.

I can't fight a man who has only one hand.

That hardened my rage; and in that instant of black wrath I lashed out and forced rapport on him; I drew into his mind roughly, with a casual swift searching that took what it wanted, then withdrew.

Stark white, shaking, Regis slumped against the railing; and I, the taste of triumph bitter on my tongue, turned my back on him. To justify my own self-contempt, I made my voice hard. "So you built the sign! You—a Hastur!"

Regis swung around, shaking with wrath. "I'd smash your face for that, if you weren't—why the hell did you *do* that?"

I said harshly, "I found out what I wanted to know."

He muttered, "You did."

Then, his eyes blazing but his voice unsteady, he said, "That's what scared me. That's why I came to you. You're an Alton, I thought you'd know. At the council, something hit me. I— I don't know anything about matrix mechanics, surely you must know that now? I don't know how I did it, or why. I just bridged the gap and threw the sign. I thought I could tell you—ask you—" His voice broke, on the ragged edge of hysteria; I heard him swear, chokingly, like a child trying not to cry. He was shaking all over.

At last he said, "All right. I'm still scared. And I could kill you for what you did. But there's no one else to ask for help." He swallowed. "What you did, you did openly. I can stand that. What I can't stand is not knowing what I might do next."

Shamed and unnerved, I walked away from him. Regis, who had tried to befriend me, had received the same treatment I'd given my worst enemy. I couldn't face him.

After a minute he followed me. "Lew. I said, we'll have to forget it. We can't afford to fight. Did it occur to you? We're both in the same fix, we're both doing things we'd never do in our right mind."

He knew, and I knew, it wasn't the same; but it made me able to look round and face him.

"Why did I do it, Lew? How, why?"

"Steady," I said. "Don't lose your head. We're all scared. I'm scared, too. But there must be a reason." I paused trying to muster my memory of the Comyn Gifts. They are mostly recessive now, bred out by intermarriage with outsiders, but Regis was physically atavistic, a throwback to the pure Comyn type; he might also be a mental throwback. "The Hastur Gift, whatever that is, is latent in you," I said. "Perhaps, unconsciously, you knew the council should be broken up, and took that drastic way of doing it." I added, diffidently, "If what had happened—hadn't happened, I'd offer to go into your mind and sift it. But—well, I don't think you'd trust me now."

"Probably not. I'm sorry."

"Don't be," I said roughly. "I don't even trust myself, after that. But Ashara or Callina, for that matter, either of the Keepers, could deep-probe and find out for you."

"Ashara—" He looked up thoughtfully toward the Keeper's Tower. "I don't know. Maybe."

We leaned across the railing, looking down into the valley, dulled now and darkened by the falling night. A baritone thunder suddenly shook the castle, and a silver dart sped bullet-wise across the sky, trailing a comet's tail of crimson, and was lost.

"Mail-rocket," I said, "from the Terran Zone."

"Terra and Darkover," said a voice behind us, "the irresistible force, and the immovable object."

Old Hastur came out on the balcony. "I know, I know," he said, "you young Altons don't like being ordered around here and there. Frankly, I don't enjoy doing it; I'm too old."

He smiled at Regis. "I sent you out to keep you from jumping into the mess along with Lew. But I wish you'd managed to keep your temper, Lew Alton!"

"*My* temper!" The unfairness of that left me speechless.

"I know. You had provocation. But if you had controlled your righteous wrath—" he spoke the words with a flavor of sour irony— "Dyan would have been clearly in the wrong. As it is—well, you broke Comyn immunity first, and that's serious. Dyan swears he'll write a writ of exile on you."

I said, almost indulgently, "He can't. The law requires at least one *laran* heir from every Domain—or why did you go to such trouble to have me recalled? I am the last living Alton, and childless. Even Dyan can't break up the Comyn that way."

Hastur scowled. "So you think you can break all our laws—being irreplaceable? Think again, Lew. Dyan swears he's found a child of yours."

"Mine? It's a stinking, sneaking lie," I said angrily. "I've lived off-world for six years. And I'm a matrix mech. You know what *that* means. And it's common knowledge I've lived celibate." Mentally I absolved myself for the single exception. If Dio had borne my child, after that summer on Vainwal, I would have known. Known? I'd have been murdered for it!

The Regent looked at me skeptically. "Yes, yes, I know. But before that? You weren't too young to be physically capable of fathering a child, were you? The child *is* an Alton, Lew."

Regis said slowly, "Your father wasn't exactly a recluse. And I suppose—how old was Marius? He might have fathered a chance-child somewhere."

I thought it over. It seemed unlikely that I should have a son. Not impossible, certainly, remembering certain adventures of my early manhood, but improbable. On the other hand, no Darkovan woman would dare swear me, or my dead kinsmen, father to her child unless she were sure past all human doubts. It takes more courage than most women have to lie about a telepath.

"And suppose I call Dyan's bluff? To produce this alleged child, prove his paternity, set him up where I am now, write his writ of exile and be damned to him? I never wanted to come back. Suppose I say go right ahead?"

"Then," said Hastur, gravely, "we'd be right back where we started." He laid his lined old hand on my arm. "Lew, I fought to have you recalled, because your father was my friend and because we Hasturs were pretty desperately outnumbered in council. I thought the Comyn needed you. Downstairs just now, when you were raking them out for their squabbles—*like children in a playground*, you said—I had high hopes. Don't make a fool of me by breaking the peace at every turn!"

I bent my head, feeling grieved and unhappy. "I'll try," I said at last, bleakly, "but by the sword of Aldones, I wish you'd left me out in space."

CHAPTER SEVEN

After the Hasturs left me, I went back to my rooms and thought over what I'd learned.

I had walked into Dyan's trap and it had snapped shut on me. I had Hastur to thank if I hadn't been already exiled. All along—I could see now—they had been goading me into open defiance. Then there was this child of mine, or my father's or Marius', a docile puppet; not a grown man with power in his own hands.

And Callina. That idea that a Keeper must be a virgin—superstitious drivel, but there must be some grain of scientific truth behind it, as with all other fables and Comyn traditions.

The superstitious could believe what they liked. But out of my own experience I knew this: any telepath working among the monitor screens will discover that his nervous and physical reflexes are all keyed into the matrix patterns. A matrix technician undergoes some prolonged periods of celibacy—strictly involuntary. This impotence is nature's safeguard. A matrix mech who upsets his nerve reactions, or through physical or emotional excesses, upsets his endocrine balance, pays for it. He can overload his nervous system to the point where he will short-circuit and blow out like a fuse; nervous depletion, exhaustion and usually death.

A woman does not have the physical safeguard of impotence. The Keepers have always been severely cloistered. Once a girl has been aroused, once that first sensual response is awakened, so disastrously physical in its effect on nerves and brain, there is no way to determine the limit of safety. For a woman the picture is black or white. Absolute chastity, or giving up her work in the screens.

I, too, must be careful; I exposed Callina to a terrible danger.

I turned around to see old Andres scowling at me; a squat, ugly Terran, fierce and surly; but I knew him too well to be deceived by his fierce looks.

I never knew how a Terran ex-spaceman had won his way into my father's confidence, but Andres Ramirez had been part of our home since I could remember. He'd taught me to ride, made toys for Marius, spanked us when we punched each other's heads or raced at too breakneck a pace, and told us endless lying tales which gave no hint about his true history. I never knew whether he could not return to Terra, or whether he would not; but twenty years dropped from my age as he growled, "What are you standing there sulking about?"

"Not sulking, damn you! Thinking!"

The old fellow snorted. "Young Ridenow is waiting to see you. You keep fine company these days!"

In the other room Lerrys stood waiting for me, tense, seemingly uneasy; his attitude made my nerves jump, but with a curt semblance of politeness, I motioned him to a seat. "If you came as Dyan's proxy, tell him not to bother. The fight's off. Hastur said so."

Lerrys sat down. "Well, no. As a matter of fact, I had a proposition for you. Has it occurred to you, now that your father's gone, you and I and Dyan are the strength of the Comyn?"

"You keep good company," I said dryly.

"Let's do without the insults. There's no reason we should fight among ourselves, there's enough for us all. You're half Terran; I suppose you have some Terran common sense. You know how the Terran Empire will handle this, don't you? They'll deal with anyone who's in a position to give orders. Why shouldn't you, and I, and Dyan, make the terms for Darkover?"

"Treason," I said slowly. "You're speaking as if the Comyn were already out of the way."

"It's bound to fall apart in a generation or two," Lerrys said quietly. "Your father, and Hastur, have been holding it together by pure force of personality for the last dozen years. You've seen Derik. Do you think he can take Hastur's place?"

I didn't. "Nevertheless," I said, "I am Comyn, and I'm vowed to stand behind Derik while he lives."

"And hold off disaster one more generation, at any cost?" Lerrys asked. "Isn't it better to make some arrangement now, rather than waiting for the big smash, and letting things lapse into anarchy for years before we can get them squared away again?"

He leaned his chin on his hands, regarding me intently. "The Terrans can do a lot for Darkover, and so can you. Listen to me, Lew. Every man has his price. I saw the way you looked at Callina today. I wouldn't touch that she-devil's fingers, let alone take her to bed, but I suppose it's a matter of taste. I thought for a while it was Dio you wanted. But you'd fit perfectly well into our plans. You'd be better than Beltran. You're educated on Terra, but you look Darkovan. You're Comyn—one of the old aristocracy. The people would accept you. You could rule the planet!"

"Under the Terrans?"

"Someone will. And if you don't—well, you're unpopular because of the Sharra rebellion. And you're Comyn. The *Terranan* make a habit of disposing of hereditary monarchies, unless they collaborate. Terra wouldn't care whether you lived or died."

Lerrys was probably right. In these days of toppling empires, no man is overburdened with loyalties. The Comyn would come crashing down eventually; why shouldn't I salvage something from the ruins?

Lerrys said, "Then you'll consider it?"

I didn't answer. A sudden intuition made me look up, and see that he had gone gray-white, his narrow fine features pinched and pale. That *bothered* me. The Ridenow are super-sensitives. In the distant past of the Comyn, when Darkover dealt with nonhumans, the Ridenow Gift had been bred into their family and they were used to detect strange presences, or give warning of unhealthy psychic or telepathic atmospheres.

He said with a strange intensity, "There are worse things than Terra, Lew. Better to make Darkover a Terran colony, even, than to face Sharra, or anything like that, from our own people."

"Erlik defend us from either!"

"The choice might be up to you, in the end."

"Hell, Lerrys, I'm not that important!"

"You may not know it," he said, "but you may be the key to everything."

Suddenly it seemed I was looking, not at one man, but at two. My brother's friend, intent on trying to get me to come over to their faction—and some deeper thing, using Lerrys for its own purpose. I was seriously debating whether I ought to turn on a damper, before he could work some mental trick on me. But I didn't move fast enough.

A flood of pure malevolence suddenly surged out of him. I jumped up, and with a terrible effort, managed to shut it out of my consciousness. Then I leaped at Lerrys, gripped him with one hand and angrily thrust my mind against his.

It wasn't Lerrys!

I met perfect, locked defense—and Lerrys alone could never have barred me from his mind. I was using a force harder than I had used on Dyan—and the Ridenow are especially vulnerable to telepathic assault. And while it did not touch whatever was using Lerrys, it tortured *him.* He writhed a moment, slumped; suddenly, frenzied into convulsions by the thing that held him, he twisted in frantic resistance. With the strength of a maniac or a berserker, he flung off my one-handed grip. And from somewhere, he found strength, too, to slam down a final defense against the assault I was using on him. Gritting my teeth in despair, I let my telepathic touch break loose. If that possessing mind should suddenly withdraw, leaving Lerrys to stand the assault alone, Lerrys would be dead or raving mad before I could get out.

Lerrys lay still, sobbing in air, for a moment. Then he sprang upright. I tensed for a renewed attack, but instead he said, quite unexpectedly, "Don't look so startled! Does it surprise you to know you're important to Darkover? Think over what I said, Lew. Your brother was a man of sense, you must have some of it too. I imagine you'll decide I'm right." Smiling in a friendly way, he held out his hand. Almost numbed, I touched his fingers, wary against some further trick.

His mind was blank, innocent of any guile, the alien gone. *He didn't even know what he had done.*

"What's the matter? You look—a bit off color," he said. "I'd put on a damper, if I were you, and get some rest. You still need it, I'd say; that blow on the head was nothing to laugh at." He bowed and went out, and I sank on a couch, wondering if the blow had, indeed, damaged my reason. *Must I be alert to attack from everyone? Or was I stark raving mad?*

A battle like that is never easy, and I was shaking in every nerve. Andres, coming through the curtains, stopped and stared in consternation.

"Get me a drink."

He started his routine protest about drinking on an empty stomach, looked at me again, stopped in mid-grumble and went. More than once I've suspected him of being more telepathic than he'll admit. When he came back it was no Darkovan cordial, but the strong Terran liquor that is sold contraband in Thendara.

I could not close my hand on the glass; to my tremendous shame, I had to lean back and let Andres hold it to my mouth. I hated the fiery stuff; but after I had swallowed a little my head cleared and I could sit up and take the glass without shaking.

"And stop trying to baby me!" I yelled at Andres, who was hovering around as if he thought I'd explode into fragments. But his familiar grumbling had a soothing effect; he'd grumbled just like this when I'd taken a tumble off my pony and broken a couple of ribs on the way down.

Just the same, I waved away his various suggestions of food and bed, and went out.

The sky was murky with traces of a storm; I could see rain squalls coming down across Nevarsin. Bad weather for the Terrans, with their dependence on planes and rockets and the shifty upper atmosphere. Our mountain-bred beasts could endure storms, blizzards, and rain. Why would a sensible people put their trust in a tricky element like the air?

I crossed the courtyard, standing at the edge of the steep embankment where the cliff fell away; a thousand feet below me, the city of Thendara lay sprawled. I leaned on the low stone wall. If one wished to attack the Terrans, one need only choose a stormy night of rain or sleet, so that their planes and rockets were laid up, to meet them on equal terms.

Behind that, the ridge of the mountains were a darker line against the dark sky, and far away, on the high slopes, I saw a gleam of fire. Some hunter's fire, perhaps; yet the glimmer reminded me that somewhere, a strange white smoke spiraled up through fires that were not ordinary flame, and an incredible tenth-level matrix twisted space around itself.

When once a man has stood at the fires of Sharra, the strange flames call to him, play on his nerves as a heavy hand sweeps harpstrings. But I knew that unless I stilled their harpings I would break completely; so I fought against the maddening live warmth that pulsed somewhere in me, reminding me of things I loathed and feared with all my heart—yet in some strange, shameful way, longed for; loved; desired.

Where could I go to still that harping?
Only to Callina.

CHAPTER EIGHT

The Aillard rooms were spacious and brilliant; shimmering walls diffused delicate colors over Callina, who knelt on the floor, playing with a little striped beast from the rainforests. It leaped on her shoulder, purring, and flickering two-toed claws in and out of her silk sleeves.

Linnell was seated near her, a harp laid flat across her knees, and Regis standing beside Linnell; but they all sensed my presence at once. Linnell put the harp aside and Callina rose hastily, putting the kitten-thing on the floor and pulling at her skirts; but I went to her and took her in my arms. She would never know how precious she had made herself to me by that glimpse of a self less guarded, less aloof. I held her a moment, then the old frustration slipped back, thrusting like an unsheathed sword between us. *Careful.*

She evaded me by speaking of Linnell. "Poor child, I'm afraid she and Derik have quarreled. She loves him—"

"It's who *you* love that interests me!" I interrupted.

She said, "I am Keeper—and *comynara!*"

"*Comynara!*" I suppose I sounded as bitter as I felt. "The Comyn would write your death warrant as soon as your marriage, if it would serve any cause!"

"If it would serve any cause, I would write my own," she said steadily. My arms strained about her.

"Are you going to let them sell you?" I flung the words at her like a curse. "What do we owe the Comyn? They've played hell with our lives since we were born!"

"Lew, I don't think you understand. I was mad, to let you think we could ever belong to each other. We can't. Not ever." Her hands went out, blindly, to push me away. "I can marry Beltran—and still keep my power to aid you, and the Comyn—because—only because I do *not* love him. Do you understand?"

I did. I let her go and stood back, looking at her in consternation. Matrix work, for a man, has its frustrating aspects. But I had never stopped to think—more accurately I had never cared a damn—what particular refinements of hellishness it might have for a woman. But before I could break out with the outrage I felt, she turned to Regis.

"Ashara has sent for us. Are you coming?"

"Not now," he said. Regis had changed, in only a few hours; he seemed older, hardened somehow. He smiled in the old easy way, but I was not wholly comfortable in his presence. It hurt to realize that Regis was keeping himself barriered from me, but in a way it was a relief.

A servant folded Callina in a wrap like a gray shadow. As we went out, and down the staircase, Linnell stood between the panels of curtain, watching us, smiling. The colored lights, spilling over her pale dress, made her a rainbow statuette in a golden aureole; suddenly, for an instant, vague unrest crystallized and fell together into one of those flashes of prevision which touch a telepath in moments of stress.

Linnell was doomed!

"Lew, what's the matter?"

I blinked. Already the certainty, that sick instant when my mind had slid off the time-track, was fading. The confusion, the sense of tragedy, remained. When I looked up again, the curtains had dropped shut and Linnell was gone.

Outside, a thin fine rain was falling. The lights had faded in the old city, dark in the lee of the cliff below; but further out, in the Terran

Zone, a neon glare of wet orange and red and green streaked the night sky with garish colors. I looked over the low wall.

"I would like to be down there tonight," I said wearily. "Or anywhere away from this hell's castle."

"Even in the Terran Zone?"

"Even in the Terran Zone."

"Why aren't you, then? No one keeps you here, if that is where you would rather be."

I turned to Callina. Her cobweb cloak spun out winglike on the wind; her hair blew, like a fine spray, about her face. I turned my back on the distant lights and pulled her close. A moment she held herself away from me, then suddenly she clung wildly, her lips frantic under mine, her arms gripping me with desperate dread. When we pulled apart, she was shaking like a young leaf.

"What now, Lew? What now?"

I gestured violently at the glare of neon. "The Terran Zone. Confront the Comyn with an accomplished fact, and let them find themselves another pawn to play with."

Slowly, the spark faded in her eyes. Turning her back on the city, she pointed at the distant ridge of the mountains, and again the illusion came: *thin white smoke, strange fire...*

"Sharra's fires burn there, still, Lew. You are no freer than I."

I put my arm around her, returning by slow degrees to sane acceptance. The rain was icy cold on our faces; we turned and went silently toward the dark mass of the tower.

The wind, broken in its sweep by the angles of the castle, flung little spits and slashes of rain at us. We passed through walled courts and pillared passages, and finally stopped before a dark arch. Callina drew me forward, and a shaft began to rise.

Ashara's Tower—so the story goes—was built for the first Keeper when Thendara was no more than a row of mud huts huddled under Nevarsin peak. It belongs to the strange days before our world writhed in earthquakes and cast off her four spinning moons. The smell of centuries hung between the musty walls with the shadows that slipped past, flitting into darkness. We rose and rose. At last the shaft halted and we stood before a carven door of glass. Not a curtain or panel of light. A door.

We stepped into blueness. Uncanny lights so mirrored and prismed the room that it seemed to have no dimension; to be at once immense and confined. The shimmer of blue glistened in the air, and under our feet; it was like swimming in blue waters or in the fire of a blue jewel.

"Come here," said a low voice, clear as winter water running under ice. "I am waiting for you."

Then and only then could my eyes focus enough in the frosty dayshine, to make out a great throne of carven glass; and the figure of a woman, seated on the throne. A straight tiny figure, almost as small as a child, in robes which so absorbed and mirrored the light that she appeared transparent.

"Ashara," I whispered, and bent my head before the Sorceress of the Comyn.

Her pale features, innocent of wrinkles as Callina's own, seemed almost fleshlessly pure. But they were old for all that, so old that even wrinkles had been smoothed away by the hand of time. The eyes, long and large, were colorless too, although in a normal light they might have been blue. There was a faint, indefinite resemblance between the two Keepers, nevertheless; as if Ashara were a stylized portrait of Callina, or Callina an embryo Ashara, not yet what Ashara was but one day to become so.

And I began to believe that she was immortal indeed, as they whispered; that she had lived on Darkover since before the coming of the Sons of Light.

She said softly, "So you have been beyond the stars, Lew Alton?"

It would not be fair to say the voice was unkind. It was not human enough for that. It only sounded as if the effort of conversing with actual, living persons, was too much for her; as if our life disturbed the cool crystalline peace that should always reign here. Callina, accustomed to this—or so I supposed—answered gently.

"You see all things, Mother. You know what we have seen."

A flicker of life crossed the ancient face. "No, not even I can see all things. And you refused my only chance to aid you, Callina. You know I have no power now, outside this place." Her voice had more vitality now, as if she were wakening to our living presence.

Callina's head bowed low. "Yet aid me with your wisdom, Ashara," she whispered. The ancient sorceress smiled remotely.

"Tell me," she said.

We sat together on a carven glass bench at Ashara's feet and told her of the events of the last few days. I asked her at last, "Can *you* duplicate the Sharra matrix?"

"Even I cannot alter the laws of matter and energy," she said. "Yet, I wish you knew less Terran science, Lew."

"Why?"

"Because, knowing, you look for explanations. Your mind would be steadier if you could call them Gods, demons, sacred talismans, as the Comyn did long ago. Sharra—a demon? No more than Aldones is a God," she said, and smiled. "Yet they are living entities, of a kind. Nor are they good or evil, though they may seem so in their contacts with men. What says the old legend?"

Callina whispered, "Sharra was bound in chains, by the Son of Hastur, who was the Son of Aldones, who was the Son of Light..."

"Ritual," I said impatiently. "Superstition!"

The still old face turned to me. "You think so? What do you know of the Sword of Aldones?"

I swallowed. "It is—the weapon against Sharra," I said. "I suppose it's a matrix, and, like the Sharra one, it's set in a sword for camouflage."

It was a hypothetical discussion anyhow, and I said so. The Sword of Aldones was in the *rhu fead*, the holy place of the Comyn, and might as well have been in another galaxy.

There are things like that on Darkover. They can't be destroyed; but they are so powerful, and so deadly dangerous, even the Comyn, or the Keepers, can't be trusted with them.

The *rhu fead* was so keyed and so activated by matrices that no one can enter it but the Comyn who have been sealed into council. It is physically impossible for an outsider to get inside without stripping his mind bare. By the time he got through the force-layer, he would be an imbecile without enough directive power to know why he had come.

But inside—the Comyn of a thousand years ago, had put them out of our own reach. They are guarded in the opposite fashion. No Comyn can touch them. An outsider could have picked them up freely, but no Comyn can come near the force-field surrounding them.

I said, "Every unscrupulous Comyn for three hundred generations has been trying to figure that one out."

"But none of them have had a Keeper on their side," Callina said. She looked at Ashara. "A Terran?"

"Perhaps," Ashara said. "At least, an outsider. Not a Terran born on Darkover, with a mind adjusted to the forces here, but a real alien. Such a one would pass where we never could. His mind would be locked off and sealed against those forces, because he wouldn't even know they were there."

"Fine," I said. "All I have to do is go some fifty light years, and bring one back, without telling him anything about this planet, or what we want him for, and hope he has enough telepathic talent to co-operate with us."

Ashara's colorless eyes held a flicker of scorn. "You are a matrix technician. What about the screen?"

Abruptly, I remembered the strange, shimmering screen I had seen in Callina's matrix laboratory. So it was one of the legendary psychokinetic transmitters, then? Vaguely, I began to see what they were aiming at. *To transmit matter, animate or inanimate, instantaneously through space—*

"That hasn't been done for hundreds of years!"

"I know what Callina can do," Ashara said with her strange smile. "Now. You and Callina touched minds, at the council—"

"Surface contact. It exhausted us both."

Ashara nodded. "Because all your energy—and hers—went into *maintaining* the contact. But I could put the two of you into focus as you and Marius were linked."

I whistled soundlessly. That was drastic; normally only the Altons can endure that deep focus.

"The Altons—and the Keepers."

I looked dubiously at Callina, but her eyes were averted. I understood; that sort of rapport is the ultimate intimacy. I wasn't any too eager myself. I had my own private hell that would not bear the light of day; could I open it for Callina's clear seeing?

Callina's hand twitched in a shuddering denial.

"No!"

The refusal hurt. If I could steel myself to this, why should she refuse?

"I will not!" There was anger in her voice, but terror, too. "I am mine—I belong to myself— No one, no one, least of all you, shall violate that!"

I was not sure whether she spoke to me or to Ashara, but I tried to calm her with tenderness. "Callina, do this for me? We can't be lovers yet, but you can belong to me this way—"

I needed her so, why did she go rigid in my arms as if my touch were shameful? She sobbed wildly, stormily. "I can't, I won't, I can't! I thought I could, but I cannot!" She faced Ashara at last, her face white, burning. "You made me so—I'd give my life if I had never seen you, I'd die to be free of you, but you made me so, and I cannot change!"

"Callina—"

"No!" Her voice vibrated with passionate refusal. "You don't know everything! You wouldn't want it, either, if you knew!"

"Enough!" Ashara's voice was a cold bell, recalling us to the silence in the tower; it seemed that even the flame in Callina's eyes died. "Be it so, then; I cannot force it. I will do what I can."

She rose from the glass throne. Her tiny, blue-ice form hardly reached to Callina's shoulder. She looked up and met my eyes for the first time; and that icy, compelling stare swallowed me...

The room vanished. For a moment I looked on blank emptiness, like the starless chasms past the rim of the universe; a shadow among shadows, I drifted in tingling mist. Then a stream of force pulsed in me; deep in my brain a spark, a core waked to life, charging me with power that stung through my whole being. I could feel myself as a network of live nerves, a sort of lacework of living force.

Then, suddenly, a face sketched itself on my mind.

I cannot describe that face, although I know, now, what it was. I saw it three times, but there are no human words to describe it. It was beautiful beyond imagining; and it was terrible beyond all conception. It was not even evil. But it was damnable and damned. Only a fraction of a second it swam in my eyes, then it burned out in the darkness. But in that instant, I looked straight in at the gates of hell.

I struggled back to reality. I was in Ashara's blue-ice tower room again. Again? Had I left it? I felt giddy and confused, disoriented; but Callina threw herself at me, and the convulsive pressure of her arms, the damp fragrance of her hair and her wet face against mine, brought me back to sanity.

Over her shoulder I saw that the carven throne was empty. "Where is Ashara?" I asked numbly.

Callina straightened, her sobs vanishing without trace. Her face held a sudden, uncanny stillness. "You had better not ask me," she murmured. "You would never believe the answer."

I frowned. I could only guess at the bond between the Keepers. Had we seen Ashara at all, or only her semblance? Had Callina seen that face?

OUTDOORS THE LIGHTS had faded; we walked through the rainy courtyard and the echoing passages without once speaking. In Callina's matrix laboratory it was warm; I pulled off my cloak, letting the heat soak into my chilled body and aching arm, while Callina busied herself adjusting the telepathic dampers. I crossed the room to the immense screen I had seen the day before, and stared, frowning, into its cloudy depths. *Transmitter.*

At its side, cradled in the silk shock-absorber, was the largest matrix I had ever seen. An ordinary matrix mechanic operates the first six levels. A telepath can manipulate the seventh and eighth. Sharra was ninth or tenth—I had never been sure—and demanded at least three linked minds, one of them a telepath. I could not even guess at the level of this one.

Sorcery? Unknown laws of science? They were one. But the freak Gift born in my blood, a spark in my nerves—I was Comyn, and for such things as this the Comyn had been bred.

To explain the screen fully would be impossible outside the Comyn. It captured images. It was a duplicator, a trap for a desired pattern. An automatic assembly of a set of predetermined requisites—no, I can't explain and I won't try.

But with my telepathic force augmented by the matrix, I could search, without space limitation, for such a mind as we wanted. Of all the billions of human and nonhuman minds in the million worlds in spacetime, somewhere was one exactly suited to our purpose, having a certain awareness—and a certain *lack* of awareness.

With the screen, we could attune that mind's vibration to *this* sector in spacetime; here, now, between the poles of the screen. Then, space annihilated by the matrix, we could shift the energons of mind and body and bring them here. My brain played with words like *hyperspace* and *dimension-travel* and *matter-transmitter,* but those were only words.

I dropped into the chair below the screen, bending to calibrate the controls to my own cerebral pattern. I fiddled fussily with the dial, not looking up. "You'll have to cut out the monitor screen, Callina."

She crossed the room and touched a series of studs; the bank of lights winked out, shunting every matrix on Darkover out of this monitor. "There's a bypass relay through the Arilinn tower," she explained.

A grill crackled and sent out a tiny staccato signal. Callina listened a moment, then said, "Yes, I know, Maruca. But we have cut out the main circuits. You'll have to hold the energons in Arilinn tonight."

She waited; then rapped out, "Put up a third-level barrier around Thendara! That is a command from Comyn; acknowledge and comply!" She turned away, sighing.

"That girl is the noisiest telepath on the planet," she said. "I wish any other Keeper had been at Arilinn tonight. There are a few who can cut through a third-level barrier, but if I asked for a fourth—" she sighed. I understood; a fourth-level barrier would have alerted every telepath on the planet to the fact that something was going on in the Comyn Castle.

We'd chance it. She took her place before the matrix, and I blanked my mind against the screen. I shut out sense impressions, reaching to adjust the psychokinetic waves into the pattern we wanted. What sort of alien would suit us? But without volition on my part, a pattern laid itself down.

I saw, in the instant before my optic nerve overloaded and went out, the dim symbols of a pattern in the matrix; then I went blind and deaf in that instant of overload that is always terrifying.

Gradually, without external senses, I found orientation in the screen. My mind, extended to astronomical proportions, swept incredible distances; traversed, in fractional seconds, whole parsecs and galaxies of subjective spacetime. There came vague touches of consciousness, fragments of thought, emotions that floated like shadows—the flotsam of the mental universe.

Then, before I felt contact, I *saw* the white-hot flare in the screen. Somewhere another mind had fitted into the pattern. We had cast it out through time and space, like a net, and when we met a mind that fitted, it had been snared.

I swung out, bodiless, divided into a billion subjective fragments, extended over a vast gulf of spacetime. If anything happened, I would never get back into my body, but would float in the spacetime curve forever.

With infinite caution, I poured myself into the alien mind. There was a short but terrible struggle; it was embedded, enlaced in mine. The world was a holocaust of molten-glass fire and color. The air writhed with cold flames, and the glow on the screen was a shadow and then a clearing darkness and then an image, captive in my mind, and then—

Light tore at my eyes. A ripping shock slammed through my brain, the floor seemed to rock and the walls to crash together and apart, and Callina was flung, reeling, against me as the energons seared the air and my brain.

Half stunned, but conscious, I looked up at Callina. The alien mind was torn free of mine. The screen was blank.

And in a crumpled heap on the floor, at the base of the screen, where she had fallen, lay a slender, dark-haired girl.

CHAPTER NINE

Unsteadily, Callina knelt beside the crumpled form. I followed slowly, and bent over beside her.

"She isn't dead?"

"Of course not." Callina looked up. "But that was terrible, even for us. What do you think it was like for her? She's in shock."

The girl was lying on her side, one arm across her face. Soft brown hair, falling forward, hid her features. I brushed it lightly back—then stopped, my hand still touching her cheek, in dazed bewilderment.

"It's Linnell," Callina choked. "Linnell!"

Lying on the cold floor was the girl on the spaceport; the girl I had seen in my first confused moments in Thendara.

For a moment, even knowing as I did what had happened, I thought my mind would give way. The transition had taken its toll of me, too. Every nerve in my body ached.

"What have we done?" Callina moaned. *"What have we done?"*

I held her tight. Of course, I thought; of course. Linnell was near; she was close to both of us; we had both been talking, and thinking of Linnell tonight. And yet...

"You know Cherillys' two point law?" I tried to put it into simple words. "Everything, everywhere, except a matrix, exists in one *exact* duplicate. This chair, my cloak, the screwdriver on your table, the public fountain in Port Chicago—everything in the universe exists in *one* exact molecular duplicate. Nothing is unique except a matrix; but there are no *three* things alike in the universe."

"Then this is—Linnell's twin?"

"More than that. Only once in a million years or so would duplicates also be twins. This is her *real* twin. Same fingerprints. Same retinal eye patterns. Same betagraphs and blood type. She won't be much like Linnell in personality, probably, because the duplicates of Linnell's environment are scattered all over the galaxy. But in flesh and blood, they're identical. Even her chromosomes are identical with Linnell's."

I took up the girl's wrist and turned it over. The curious matrix mark of the Comyn was duplicated there. "Birthmark," I said, "but the effect is identical in her flesh. See?"

I stood up. Callina stared and stared. "Can she live in this environment, then?"

"Why not? If she's Linnell's duplicate, she breathes oxygen in the same ratio we do, and her internal organs are adjusted to about the same gravity."

"Can you carry her? She'll get another bad shock if she wakes up in this place!" Callina indicated the matrix equipment.

I grinned humorlessly. "She'll get one anyway." But I managed to scoop her up, one-armed. She was frail and light, like Linnell. Callina held curtains aside for me, showed me where to lay her. I covered the girl, for it was cold, and Callina murmured, "I wonder where she comes from?"

"She was born on a world with gravity about the same as Darkover, which narrows it considerably. Vialles, Wolf, even Terra. Or, of course, some planet we never heard of." Her speech had impressed me as Terran; but I hadn't told Callina about that episode on the spaceport, and didn't intend to. "Let's leave her to sleep off the shock, and get some sleep ourselves."

Callina stood in the door with me, her hands locked on mine. She looked haggard and worn, but lovely to me after the shared danger, shared weariness. I bent and kissed her.

"Callina," I whispered. It was half a question, but she freed her hand gently and I did not press her. She was right. We were both desperately exhausted. It would have been raving insanity. I put her gently away and went out without looking back. It was raining hard, but until the wet red morning rose sunlessly over Thendara I paced the courtyard, restless, and the drops on my face were not all rain.

Toward dawn I fought back to self-control, and went back to the Keeper's Tower. I was afraid that without Callina at my side I would not find a way into the blue-ice room, or that Ashara had vanished into some inaccessible place. But she was there; and such was the illusion of the frosty light, or of my tired eyes, that she seemed younger, less guarded; like a strange, icy, inhuman Callina. My brain almost refused to think clearly, but I finally managed to formulate my plea.

"You can see—time. Tell me. The child Dyan calls mine—"

"It is yours," Ashara said.

"Who—"

"I know. You've been celibate, except for Diotima Ridenow, since your Marjorie died." She looked right through my astonished stare. "No, I didn't read your mind, I thought the Ridenow girl might be suitable to train as I—as I trained Callina. She was not. I'm not concerned with your moralities or Diotima's; it's a matter of physical nerve alignments." She went on, passionlessly, "Hastur would not accept the bare word of those who brought the child; so he brought her to my keeping for search. She is here in the Tower. You may see her. She is yours. Come with me."

To my surprise—I don't know why, but somehow I had felt that Ashara could not leave her strange blue-ice room—she led me through another of the bewildering blue doors and into a plain circular room. One of the furry nonhuman mutes—the servants of the Keeper's Tower—scurried away on noiseless padded feet.

In the cool normal light Ashara's flickering figure was colorless, almost invisible. I wondered; was it the sorceress herself, or merely a projection she wanted me to see? The room was simply furnished, and on a narrow white cot at the center, a little girl lay fast asleep. Pale reddish-gold hair lay scattered on the pillow.

I went slowly to the child, and looked down. She was very small; five or six, maybe younger. And as I looked down I knew they had told the truth. In ways impossible to explain, except to a telepath and an Alton, I knew; this was my own child, born of my own seed. The tiny triangular face bore not the slightest resemblance to my own; but my blood knew. Not my father's. Not my brother's. My own. My flesh.

"Who was her mother?" I asked softly.

"You'll be happier all your life if I never tell you."

"I can take it! Some light woman of Carthon or Daillon?"

"No."

The child murmured, stirred and opened her eyes. I took one step toward her—then turned, in an agony of appeal, on Ashara. Those eyes, those eyes, gold-flecked amber... "Marjorie," I said hoarsely, painfully, "Marjorie died, she *died*...

"She is not Marjorie Scott's daughter." Ashara's voice was clear, cool, pitiless. "Her mother was Thyra Scott."

"Thyra?" I fought an insane impulse to laugh. "Thyra? That's impossible! I never—I wouldn't have touched that she-devil's fingertips, much less—"

"Nevertheless, this is your child. And Thyra's. The details are not clear to me. There is a time—I am not sure. They may have had you drugged, hypnotized. Perhaps I could find out. It would not be easy, even for me. That part of your mind is a closed and sealed room. It does not matter."

I shut my teeth on a black, sickening rage. *Thyra!* That red hellion, so like and so unlike Marjorie, perfect foil for Kadarin! What had they done? How—

"It does not matter. It is your child."

Resentfully, accepting the fact, I glowered at the little girl. She sat up, tense as a scared small animal, and it wrenched at me with sudden hurt. *I had seen Marjorie look like that. Small, scared. Lost and lonesome.*

I said, as gently as I could, "Don't be afraid of me, *chiya,* I'm not a very pretty sight, but I don't eat little girls."

The little girl smiled. The small pointed face was suddenly charming; a tiny gnome's grin marred by a dimple. There were twin gaps in the straight little teeth.

"They said you were my father."

I turned, but Ashara was gone, leaving me alone with my unexpected daughter. I sat down uneasily on the edge of the cot. "So it would seem. How do they call you, *chiya?*"

"Marja," she said shyly. "I mean Marguerhia—" she lisped the name, Marjorie's name, in the odd old-world dialect still heard in the mountains sometimes. "Marguerhia Kadarin, but I just be Marja." She knelt upright, looking me over. "Where is your other hand?"

I laughed uneasily. I wasn't used to children. "It was hurt and they had to take it off."

Her amber eyes were enormous. She snuggled against my knee, and I put my arm around her, still trying to get it clear in my mind.

Thyra's child. Thyra Scott had been Kadarin's wife—if you could call it that. But everyone knew he was rumored to be half-brother to the Scotts, Zeb Scott's child by one of the half-human mountain things. Back in the Hellers, half-brothers and sisters sometimes married; and it was not uncommon for such a marriage to adopt the child of one by someone else, thus avoiding the worst consequences of too much inbreeding. I scowled, trying to penetrate the gray murk which surrounded part of the Sharra affair in my mind. I had never probed that partial amnesia; I had felt, instinctively, that madness might lie there.

Perhaps I had been drugged with aphrosone. I knew how that worked. The one drugged lives a life outwardly normal, but he himself knows nothing of what he does, losing continuity of thought between each breath. Memory is retained in symbolic dreams; a psychiatrist, hearing what was dreamed during the time spent under aphrosone, can unravel the symbols and tell the victim what really happened. I had never wanted to know. I didn't now.

"Where were you brought up, Marja?"

"In a big house with a lot of other little girls and boys," she said. "*They're* orphans. I'm not. I'm something else. Matron says it's a wicked word I must never, *never* say, but I'll whisper it to you."

"Don't." I winced slightly; I could guess.

And Lawton, in the Trade City, had told me; *Kadarin never goes anywhere—except to the spaceman's orphanage.*

Marja put her head sleepily on my shoulder. I started to lay her down. Then I felt a curious stir and realized, abruptly, that the child had reached out and made contact with my mind!

The thought was staggering. Amazed, I stared at the tiny girl. Impossible! Children do not have telepathic power—even Alton children! Never!

Never? I couldn't say that; obviously, Marja *did* have it. I caught my arms around her; but I broke the contact gently, not knowing how much she could endure.

But one thing I *did* know. Whoever had the legal right of it, this little girl was *mine*! And no one and nothing was going to keep her from me. Marjorie was dead; but Marja lived, whoever her parents, with Marjorie's face sketched in her features, the child Marjorie would have borne me if she had lived, and the rest was better forgotten. And if anyone—Hastur, Dyan, Kadarin himself—thought they could keep my daughter from me, they were welcome to try!

Dawn was paling outside the tower, and abruptly I was conscious of exhaustion. I had had quite a night. I laid Marja down in the cot; drew up the warm covers under her chin. She looked up at me wistfully, without a word.

On an impulse I bent and hugged her. "Sleep well, little daughter," I said, and went very softly out of the room.

CHAPTER TEN

The next day, Beltran of Aldaran, with his mountain escort, came to the Comyn Castle.

I had not wanted to be present at the ceremonies which welcomed him; but Hastur insisted and I finally agreed. I'd have to meet Beltran sometime. It had better be among strangers where we could both be impersonal.

He greeted me with some constraint; we had once been friends, but the past lay between us, with its grim shadow of blood. I was grateful for the set phrases of custom; I could mouth them without examining them for a hostility I dared not show.

Beltran presented me, ceremoniously, to some of his escort. A few of them remembered me from years ago; but I looked away as I met a dark familiar face.

"You remember Rafael Scott," Beltran of Aldaran said.

I did.

There is no such word as endless, or the ceremonies would still be going on. However, at last Beltran and his people were handed over to servants, to be shown to rooms, fed, and permitted to recuperate for the further formalities of the evening. As we dispersed. Rafe Scott followed me from the hall, and I turned to him brusquely.

"Listen, you," I said, "you're here under Beltran's safe-conduct, and I can't lay a hand on you. But I warn you—"

"What the hell's the *matter*?" he demanded. "Didn't Marius explain? Where is Marius, anyhow?"

I looked at him, bitterly. This time I would not be taken in by the confiding manner that had gulled me before, when I was sick from space and too trusting to doubt him.

He laid rough hands on me. "Where's Marius, damn you!"

It got to him, through the touch. He let me go and fell back. "Dead! Oh, no— *no!*" He covered his face with his hands, and this time I could not doubt his sincerity. That momentary shock of rapport had at least convinced us that we were telling the truth to each other.

His voice was not steady when he spoke. "He was my friend, Lew. The best friend I had. May I die in Sharra's fire if I had a hand in it."

"Can you blame me for doubting you? You were the only one who knew I had the Sharra matrix, and they killed him to get it."

He said evenly, "Believe what you like, but I haven't seen Kadarin twice in the last year." His face was wrung with grief. "Didn't Marius ever get a chance to explain it to you? Damn it, if I wanted to hurt him, would I have loaned him my pistol? He gave it to the Ridenow boy—Lerrys—because he was afraid to take it into the Terran Zone. Like I said, it has the contraband mark on it. I have a permit but he didn't. When you thought I was Marius, I pretended—I thought, if I could only get a chance to keep the two of you apart, until you understood what was going to happen—"

I could not disbelieve his sincerity. After a moment I put my hand on his shoulder. Had we been Darkovan men, we would have embraced and wept; but we both have the reserve of our Terran blood. I said baldly, at last, "You have seen Kadarin?"

"A few times, with Thyra. I've tried to keep out of his way." Rafe looked at me, oddly. "Oh, I see. They've told you about her baby."

"And mine," I said grimly. "I imagine I was drugged with aphrosone. Why did she do it?"

"I don't know," Rafe said. "Thyra never tells anyone anything. There's an odd streak in Thyra—almost inhuman. She's very strange with the baby too. In the end Bob had to put the kid in the spaceman's orphanage. He didn't want to. He loved the kid."

"And knew she was mine?" It didn't make sense, any of it. Least of all that a child of mine had grown up to call Kadarin father, to bear his name, to love him.

"Of course he knew. How could he help it? I think he made Thyra do it," Rafe said. "He's had Marja home a dozen times, but he couldn't keep her. Thyra—"

But before he could go on, we were interrupted by a palace servant with a message from Callina.

"We'll talk again," Rafe said, as I took my leave. And I was not sure whether it was a promise or a threat.

CALLINA LOOKED TIRED and harried.

"The girl's awake," she greeted me. "She was hysterical when she came to; I gave her a sedative, and she's calmed down a little. Lew, what are we going to do now?"

"I won't know until I see her," I said emptily.

The girl had been moved to a spacious room in the Aillard apartments. When we came in, she was lying across a bed, her face buried in the covers; but it was a tearless and defiant face she raised to me.

She was still Linnell's double. She looked more so, having been decently dressed in Darkovan clothing, which I supposed—correctly—to be Linnell's own.

"Please tell me the truth," she said steadily. "Where am I? Oh—" she cried out, and hid her face. "The man with one hand who kissed me on the spaceport, back on Darkover!"

Callina stood apart, a figure of dignified disdain, leaving me to squirm alone. "That was a— a mistake," I said lamely. "Allow me to introduce myself. Lew Alton-Comyn, z'par servu. And you?"

"That's the first sensible thing anyone has said." Although she spoke the language badly, I was amazed at the luck that gave us someone who could speak it at all. "Kathie Marshall."

"Terranan?"

"Terran, yes. Are you Darkovan? What's all this?"

"I suppose we do owe you an explanation," I said, and broke off, staring with what I suppose must have been a very stupid expression. "But I'm damned if I know how to explain it!"

"You have nothing to fear. We brought you here because we need your help—"

"But why me? Where's here? And what makes you think I'd help you, even if I could—after you've kidnapped me?"

It was, I supposed, a fair question.

Callina said, "Shall we bring Linnell here, and let her see? You were brought here, Kathie, because you are twinned in mind with my sister Linnell. We had to—take the chance that you would be willing to help us, but there will be no compulsion involved. And no one will hurt you."

As Callina moved toward her, Kathie sprang up and backed away. "Twinned minds? That's—that's ridiculous! Where am I?"

"In the Comyn Castle in Thendara."

"Thendara? But that's—that's on *Darkover!* I— I left Darkover weeks ago. I arrived on Samarra just last night. No," she said, "no, I'm dreaming. I saw you on Darkover and I'm *dreaming* about you!" She went to the window and I saw her white hands clench on a fold of curtain. "A— a *red* sun— Darkover—oh, I have dreams like this when I can't wake up. I can't wake up—" She was so deathly white that I thought she would faint. Callina came and put an arm around her, and this time Kathie did not pull away.

"Try to believe us, my child," Callina said. "You are on Darkover. Have you heard anything of matrix mechanics? We brought you here like that." It was a grossly inaccurate description, but it calmed her somehow.

"Who are you, then?"

"Callina Aillard. Keeper of the Comyn."

"I've heard about the Keepers," Kathie said shakily. "Look, you—you *can't* take a Terran citizen, and—and pull her halfway across the Galaxy; my father's going to tear the planet apart looking for me—" Her voice broke and she covered her face with her hands. She was only a child. From the child came the scared wail. "I'm afraid! I— I want to go home!"

Gently, as she might have spoken to Linnell herself, Callina murmured, "Poor child! Don't be frightened!"

There was something else I had to do. Kathie must keep her immunity, and unawareness, of Darkovan forces. I knew one way to do that. Yet I hated doing it; I must make myself vulnerable. In effect, I meant to put a barrier around her mind; built into the barrier would be a sort of bypass circuit, so that any attempt to make telepathic contact with Kathie, or dominate her mind, would be immediately shunted from her open mind to my guarded one.

There was no sense in explaining to Kathie what I meant to do. While she clung to Callina, I reached out as gently as I could and made contact with her.

It was an instant of screaming pain in every nerve. Then it blanked out, and Kathie was sobbing convulsively. "What did you *do*? Oh, I felt you—but no, that's crazy. What are you?"

"Why couldn't you wait till she understood?" Callina demanded. But I stood looking at them somberly, without answering. I had done what I had to do, and I had done it *now*, because I wanted Kathie safely barriered before anyone saw her and guessed. And, above all, before Callina confronted her with Linnell. That moment of prevision last night had left me desperately uneasy. Why, of all the patterns in the world, why Linnell?

What happened when a pair of exact duplicates met? I couldn't remember ever hearing.

It hurt to see her cry; she was so like Linnell, and Linnell's tears had always upset me. Callina looked up helplessly, trying to soothe the weeping girl. "You had better go away for now," she said, and as Kathie's sobs broke out afresh, "Go *away*! I'll handle this!"

I shrugged, suddenly angry. "As you please," I said and turned my back on them. Why couldn't she trust me?

And that moment, when I left Callina in anger, was the moment when I snapped the trap shut on us all.

CHAPTER ELEVEN

Once in every journey of Darkover around its sun, the Comyn, city folk, mountain lords, off-world consuls and ambassadors and Terrans from the Trade City, mingled together in carnival with a great outward show of cordiality. Centuries ago, this festival had merely brought Comyn and commoner together. Now it involved everyone of any importance on the planet; and the festival opened with the display of dancing in the great lower halls of the Comyn Castle.

Centuries of tradition made this a masked affair; in compliance with custom, I wore a narrow half-mask, but had made no further attempt at disguise. I stood at one end of the long hall, talking indifferently and listening with half an ear to a couple of youngsters in the Terran space service, and as soon as I decently could, I got away and stood staring out at the four miniature moons that had nearly floated into conjunction over the peak.

Behind me the great hall blazed with colors and costumes that reflected every corner of Darkover and almost every known form of human or half-human life throughout the Terran Empire. Derik glittered in the golden robes of an Arturian sun-priest; Rafe Scott had assumed the mask, whip and clawed gloves of a *kifirgh* duelist.

In the corner reserved, by tradition, for young girls, Linnell's spangled mask was a travesty of disguise, and her eyes were glowing with happy consciousness of all the eyes on her. As *comynara*, she was known to everyone on Darkover; but she rarely saw anyone outside the narrow circle of her cousins and the few selected companions permitted to a girl of the Comyn hierarchy. Now, masked, she could speak to, or even dance with, perfect strangers, and the excitement of it was almost too much for her.

Beside her, also masked, I recognized Kathie. I didn't know why she was here, but I saw no harm in it. She was safely barricaded by the by-pass circuit I had built into her mind; and there was, probably, no better way of proving that she was not a prisoner, but an honored guest. From her resemblance to Linnell, they'd only think her some noble-woman of the Aillard clan.

Linnell laughed up at me as I joined them; "Lew, I am teaching your cousin from Terra some of our dances! Imagine, she didn't know them."

My cousin. I suppose that was Callina's idea. Anyway, it explained her badly accented Darkovan. Kathie said gently, "I wasn't taught to dance, Linnell."

"Not taught to dance? But what did you learn, then?" Linnell asked incredulously. "Don't they dance on Terra, Lew?"

"Dancing," I said dryly, "is an integral part of all human cultures. It is a group activity passed down from the group movements of birds and anthropoids, and also a social channeling of mating behavior. Among such quasi-human races as the *chieri* it becomes an ecstatic behavior pattern akin to drunkenness. Men dance on Terra, on Megaera, on Vainwal, and in fact, from one end of the civilized Galaxy to the other, as far as I know. For further information, lectures on anthropology are given in the city; I'm not in the mood."

I turned to Kathie in what I hoped was properly cousinly fashion; "Suppose we do it instead?"

I added to Kathie, as we danced, "Of course you wouldn't know that dancing is a major study with children here. Linnell and I both learned as soon as we could walk. I had only the public instruction, but Linnell has been studying ever since." I glanced affectionately back at

Linnell. "I went to a dance or two on Terra. Do you think our Darkovan ones are so different?"

I was studying the Terran girl rather closely. Why would a duplicate of Linnell have the qualities we needed for the work in hand? Kathie, I realized, had guts and brains and tact; it took them, to come here after the shock she had had, and play the part tacitly assigned to her. And Kathie had another rare quality. She seemed unconscious that my left arm, circling her waist, was unlike anyone else's. I've danced with girls on Terra. It's not common.

With seeming irrelevance, Kathie said, "How sweet Linnell is! It's as if she were really my twin; I loved her, the minute I saw her. But I'm afraid of Callina. It's not that she's unkind—no one could have been kinder! But she doesn't seem quite human. Please, let's not dance? On Terra I'm supposed to be a good dancer, but here I feel like a stumbling elephant."

"You probably weren't taught as intensively." That, to me, was the oddest thing about Terra—the casualness with which they regarded this one talent which distinguishes man from four-footed kind. Women who could not dance! How could they have true beauty?

I just happened to be watching the great central curtains when they parted and Callina Aillard entered the hall. And for me, the music stopped.

I have seen the black night of interstellar space flecked by single stars. Callina was like that, in a scrap torn from the midnight sky, her dark hair netted with pale constellations.

"How beautiful she is," Kathie whispered. "What does the dress represent? I've never seen one just like it."

"I don't know," I said. But I lied. I did not know why any girl on the eve of her marriage—even an unwilling marriage—should assume the traditional costume of *la damnée:* Naotalba, daughter of doom, bride of the daemon Zandru. What would happen when Beltran caught the significance of the costume? A more direct insult would have been hard to devise—unless she had come in the dress of the public hangman!

I excused myself quickly from Kathie and went toward Callina. She had agreed to the wishes of the Comyn; she had no right to embarrass her family like this, at such a late date. But by the time I reached her, she was already getting that lecture from old Hastur; I caught the tail of it.

"Behaving like a naughty, willful child!"

"Grandfather," said Callina, in that quiet, controlled voice, "I will neither look nor act a lie. This dress pleases me. It is perfectly suited to the way I have been treated by the Comyn all my life." Her laugh was musical and unexpectedly bitter. "Beltran of Aldaran would endure more insults than this—for *laran* rights in council! You will see." She turned away from the old man.

"Dance with me, Lew?"

It was no request but a command; as such I obeyed, but I was upset and didn't care if she knew it. It was shameful, to spoil Linnell's first dance like this!

"I am sorry, about Linnell," Callina said. "But the dress pleases my mood. And it is becoming, is it not?"

It was. "You're too damned beautiful," I said hoarsely. "Callina, Callina, you're *not* going through with this—this crazy farce!" I drew her into a recess and bent to kiss her, savagely crushing my mouth on hers. For a moment she was passive, startled; then went rigid, bending back and pushing me frantically away. "No! Don't!"

I let my arms drop and stood looking at her, slow fury heating my face. "That's not the way you acted last night!"

She was almost weeping. "Can't you spare me this?"

"Did you ever think there were things you might have spared me? Farewell, Callina *comynara;* I wish Beltran joy of his bride." I felt her catch at my sleeve, but I shook her off and strode away.

I skirted the floor, grimly quiet. A nagging unease, half telepathic, beat on me. Aldaran was dancing with Callina now; viciously I hoped he'd try to kiss her. Lerrys, Dyan? They were in costume, unrecognizable. Half the Terran colony could be here, too, and I'd never know.

Rafe Scott was chatting with Derik in a corner; Derik looked flushed, and his voice, when he turned and greeted me, was thick and unsteady. "Eve'n, Lew."

"Derik, have you seen Regis Hastur? What's his costume?"

"Do' know," Derik said thickly. "I'm Derik, tha's all I know. Have 'nough trouble rememberin' that. You try it some time."

"A fine spectacle," I muttered. "Derik, I wish you would remember who you are! Get out and sober up, won't you? Do you realize what a show you are giving the Terrans?"

"I think—forget y'self," he mumbled. "Not your affair wha' I do—ain' drunk anyhow."

"Linnell should be very proud of you!" I snapped.

"Li'l girl's mad at me." He forgot his anger and spoke in a tone of intimate self-pity. "Won't even dansh—"

"Who would?" I muttered, standing on both feet so I would not kick him. I resolved to hunt up Hastur again; he had authority I didn't, and influence with Derik. It was bad enough to have a Regency in such times. But when the heir presumptive makes a public idiot of himself before half a planet!

I scanned the riot of costumes, looking for Hastur. One in particular caught my eye; I had seen such harlequins in old books on Terra. Parti-colored, a lean beaked cap over a masked face, gaunt and somehow horrible. Not in itself, for the costume was only grotesque, but there was a sort of atmosphere, the man himself—I scowled, angry at myself. Was I imagining things already?

"No. I don't like him either," said Regis quietly at my side. "And I don't like the atmosphere of this room—or this night." He paused. "I went to grandfather today, and demanded *laran.*"

I gripped his hand, without a word. Every Comyn comes to that, soon or late.

"Things are different," he said slowly. "Maybe I'm different. I know what the Hastur Gift is, and why it's recessive in so many generations. I wish it was as recessive in me as in grandfather."

I didn't have to answer. He would heal. But now that new strength, that added dimension—whatever it was—was a raw wound in his brain.

He said, "You remember about the Hastur and Alton Gifts? How tight can you barrier your mind? Hell could break loose, you know."

"In a crowd like this, my barriers aren't worth too much," I said. I knew what he meant, though. The Hastur and Alton Gifts were mutually antagonistic, the two like poles of a magnet which cannot be made to touch. I didn't know what the Hastur Gift was; but from time immemorial in the Comyn, Hastur and Alton could work together only with infinite precaution—even in the matrix screens. Regis, a latent Hastur, his Gift dormant, I could join in rapport; could even force it on him undesired. A developed Hastur, which he had suddenly become, could knock my mind from his with the fury of lightning. Regis and I could read each other's minds if we wanted to—ordinary telepathy isn't affected—but we could probably never link in rapport again.

Reluctantly I found myself wondering. I had forced contact on Regis; had he taken this step to protect himself from another such attempt? Didn't he trust me?

But before I could ask him, the dome lights were switched off. Immediately the room was flooded with streaming, silvery moonlight; there was a soft "A—ah!" from the thronged guests as, through the clearing dome, the four moons, blazing now in full conjunction, lighted the floor like daylight. Suddenly, I felt a light touch, and looked down to see Dio Ridenow standing beside me.

Her dress—a molded tabard of some stuff that gleamed, green and blue and silver, in the shifting moonlight—was so breathtakingly fitted to her body that it might as well have been sprayed on; and her fair hair, the color of the moonlight, rippled like water with the glint of jewels. She tossed her head, with a little silvery chiming of tiny bells.

"Well? Am I beautiful enough for you?"

I tried to sidestep the provocative tone, the green witch-fire in her saucy eyes. "I must say it is an improvement over your riding breeches," I said dryly.

She giggled and tucked her hand through my arm; a hard, light little hand. "Dance with me, Lew? A secain?" Without waiting for my answer, she tapped the rhythm-pattern on the light-panel, and after a moment the steady, characteristic beat of the secain throbbed into the invisible music.

The secain is no formal promenade. Last year Dio and I had outraged the dowagers and the dandies, even on the pleasure-world of Vainwal, by dancing it there. I didn't want to dance it here. The floor was almost cleared now; most of the Thendara women are too prim for this wild and ancient mountain dance.

Still, I owed Dio something.

For a Darkovan girl, Dio was not a particularly expert dancer. But she was warm and vibrant; she smiled teasingly up at me, and, resenting that smile which took so much for granted, I whirled her till another girl would have screamed for mercy. But as she came upright she laughed at me; as always, she was scornful of my strength. She was like spring-steel tempered to my touch.

In the last figure of the dance I caught her tighter than the pattern of the dance demanded. This we had come to know well, this sense of being in key, body and mind, a closer touch than any physical intimacy. The beat of the secain throbbed in my blood, and as the music pulsed and pounded to climax, my senses pounded and pulsed, and as the final explosive drum-and-cymbal chord quivered and rang, I kissed her—hard.

The silence was anticlimax. Dio slid from my arms, and under the softening music we passed out under the open sky.

"I've been wondering—" teasingly, Dio lowered her voice, "when Hastur told you about your child—did you wonder about me?"

I frowned, displeased. That came too close for comfort. She laughed, but the laugh was sharp and mirthless.

"Thanks. I wasn't, if that helps any. Lew—do you really want that girl Callina?"

This I would not discuss with Dio.

"Why? Do you care?"

"Not much." But it didn't sound convincing. "But I think you're a fool. After all, she's not a woman—"

Now I was really shocked. This was not like Dio. I said, angrily, "As much as yourself!"

"That's almost funny, coming from you!"

I threatened, "Dio, if you make a scene, I will find it a pleasure to break your neck."

"I know you will!" She was laughing again, but this time it was high and hysterical. "That's what I love about you! Your solution for all problems! Kill someone! Break a neck or two! But one thing I know, for sure; Callina's finished, and Ashara's going to lose her pawn!"

"What the devil are you talking about?"

She was still laughing that wildly hysterical laughter. "You'll see! It could have been you, you know, you could have saved them all that trouble! You and your crazy scruples! You cheated yourself, and especially Callina! Or, should I say, you played Ashara's game—"

I caught her wrist with the trick hold I'd used on Regis and wrenched her abruptly round. My fingers crushed on her wrist till she writhed, "You brute, you're breaking my arm! Damn it, Lew, you're not funny, you're *hurting* me!"

"You ought to be hurt," I said savagely. "You ought to be beaten! *What are they going to do to Callina?* Tell me, or I swear, Dio, I've never used the Gift on a woman before, but I'll tear it out of you if I have to!"

"You couldn't!" We were facing each other now in a blaze of fury that obliterated everything outside. "Remember?"

"Damn you!" The truth made me savage. Dio alone of all people was completely and perfectly protected against my Gift, forever—because of what had been between us on Vainwal. It had to be that way.

There are things no telepath, no man, can control. That—touching—in intimacy, is one of them. And Dio was one of the hypersensitive Ridenow. To safeguard her sanity, I had given her certain defenses against me. I could never take more from her, telepathically, than she wanted to give. More was impossible. I could remove that barrier—if I wanted to kill her. No other way.

I swore, impotently. Suddenly Dio flung her arms around my neck, eyes burning at me like green flames. "You blind fool," she choked, "you can't see what's before your very eyes, and you'll go blundering in again and spoil it all! Can't you trust me?"

She was very close, and the contact was dizzying. Realizing what she was doing, I thrust her suddenly and roughly away. "That won't get you anywhere."

Her face hardened. "Very well. There is a rumor current—and believed—that only a virgin may hold Callina's particular powers. There is, shall I say, a certain faction which holds to the belief that we would all be better off if Callina were—let's say—made suddenly powerless. And since your conduct is above reproach, there is *one* way to remedy the situation—"

I stared at her, dimly beginning to realize what she meant. But that was horrible! And was there any man on Darkover who would dare— "Dio, if this is your idea of a filthy joke—"

"A joke, but it's on Ashara," she said. Suddenly she grew quiet and deadly serious. "Lew, trust me. I can't explain, but you've got to keep out of it. Callina isn't what you think, not at all. She isn't—"

I brought my hand back and slapped her, hard. The blow sent her reeling. "You've had that coming for a year," I grated.

Suddenly Regis was close beside me; in an instant he had caught the overflowing of my thought, and his face paled. "Callina!"

Dio stood holding her cheek where I had slapped her, staring open-mouthed; but she threw herself forward on me now. "Wait," she begged, "Wait, you don't understand—"

I thrust her aside, swearing. Regis kept pace with me. Finally he breathed, "But who would dare? A Keeper, remember—actually to lay hands on her?"

I stopped. "Dyan," I said at last, quietly. "What did she say, in council? No man lives to maul me *three* times. If that were the first—"

We were in light surface contact. Abruptly I stopped him; he looked at me grimly and the touch of his mind fell from mine as clasped hands loosen.

"I thought so," I said. "When we touch, all the strength drains out of us both. They've smuggled some trap-matrix in there, eighth or ninth level, the kind that picks up vital energy—" My jaw fell. "Sharra!"

"Lew, are we *feeding* that damned thing?"

"We'll hope not," I said. "Can you touch Callina?"

I felt Regis, almost instinctively, grope for contact again; quickly, I barricaded myself. "Don't ever do that!" I commanded. The fumbling touch was raw agony; yet endure it I must, danger or no, at least once more. "Regis, when I say the word, link with me—for about a thousandth of a second. But whatever you do, don't freeze into rapport with me! If you do, we'll both burn out. Remember, you're Hastur and I'm Alton!"

He swallowed, convulsively. "You'd better do the linking. I can't control it yet."

For the barest instant, then, we contacted, in a scanning that sifted the whole diameter of the crowd. It was not a hundredth of a second, but even that flung us apart in a shock of blinding pain. A full tenth of a second would have burned out every spark of vital energy in our bodies. To whoever controlled the hidden matrix, it must have flamed like a starship on a radar screen.

But I knew what I wanted. Somewhere in the castle, a trap-matrix—not Sharra this time—was focused, with obscene intensity, on the weakest link in the Comyn: Derik Elhalyn.

And I had thought him only drunk!

The thick, inarticulate speech; the irritable confusion of brain, the fumbling limbs—all symptoms of a mind under an unmonitored matrix. And whoever set it, had a mind both perverted and sadistic—that this complex revenge on Callina should be carried out by Linnell's lover!

I reached for Callina, but only emptiness greeted my seeking mind. It is a horrifying thing to feel only an empty place in the fluid mechanism of space, where once there was a living mind. Could even death blank her away so completely?

Regis turned a strained, heartbroken face to me.

"Lew, if he's touched her—"

"Easy. Derik doesn't know, he never will know what he's doing, you know. Listen; I need your help. I'm going straight into Derik's mind and try to lift the matrix trap." For the first time in my life I was grateful for the Alton Gift, which could force rapport—and which could go into a matrix without the half-dozen monitors and dampers an ordinary matrix mech would need. "Those things are plain hell, Regis. Now, when I get it lifted, you try to break it up. But don't you touch me—or Derik—or you'll kill all three of us."

It was a desperate chance. No sane person will go into a mind controlled by a trap-matrix; it is walking into a blind alley which may be filled with monsters ready to spring. And I would have to drop all my barriers, and trust the untried strength of a newly-*laran* Hastur who could kill me with a random touch.

Every instinct screamed no; but I reached out and focused on Derik.

And knew, at once, I had touched that thing before; when I tried to probe Lerrys.

Derik, like a man who feels the sting of a knife through an incomplete anesthetic, twisted to escape; but this time I held fast, grimly, forcing my focused strength as a wedge between mind and the trick matrix that held it in submission.

Behind me, as a man may look at mirrored light he dares not face, I sensed Regis; he had seized on that alien force, and he was tearing it to bits; destroying each strand of force as I lifted that telepathic web, thread by thread, out of the nerves of Derik's brain.

But now it was being forced on me, too. As a man at a screen may watch two starships battle, so the holder of this unholy matrix was watching the three-way duel, perhaps ready with a new weapon. Necessity and the need for haste made me careless how I tortured Derik; but I knew, too, if Derik were himself, he would thank me for this.

As I forced down barrier after barrier, something fought me, a grotesque parody of the real Derik; but I won. I felt it flicker, vanish like a trace of smoke, burnt away. The compulsion was gone, the trap-matrix destroyed—and Derik, at least, was clean.

I withdrew.

Regis leaned against a pillar, his face dead white. I asked, "Could you tell who was controlling it?"

"Not a trace. When the matrix shattered, I felt Callina, but then—" Regis frowned, "she blanked again, and all I felt, was *Ashara*! Why Ashara?"

I didn't know. But if Ashara were aroused and aware, at least she would protect Callina.

We had given ourselves away, Regis and I; we had lost vital strength; but for the moment, perhaps, we were safe. My main worry now was for Regis. I was mature, trained in the use of these powers, and I knew the limits of my own endurance. He didn't. Unless he learned caution, the next step would be nerve depletion and collapse.

I tried to warn him, but he shrugged it off. "Don't worry about me. Who's that with Linnell?"

I turned to see if he meant Kathie or the man in harlequin costume who had so disturbed me. Beside them was another masked figure, a man in a cowled robe which hid his face and body completely. But something about him reminded me, suddenly and horribly, of the hell in Derik's mind. Another victim—or the controller? I had to fight myself to keep from running across the room and pitching him bodily away from Linnell.

I went toward them, slowly. Linnell asked, "Lew, where have you been?"

"Outside, watching the sky," I said briefly.

Linnell glanced up at me, timidly, troubled.

"What is it, *chiya?*" The childish pet name still came easily.

"Lew, who is Kathie, really? When I'm near her, I feel terribly strange. It's not just because she *looks* so like me, it's as if she *were* me. And then I feel—I don't know—as if I had to come close to her, touch her, embrace her. It's a kind of pain! I can't keep away from her! But if I do touch her, I want to pull away and scream—" Linnell was twisting her hands nervously, ready to burst into hysterical tears or laughter. I didn't know what to say. Linnell wasn't a girl to fret over trifles; if it affected her like this, it was no minor whim.

Kathie had been dancing with Rafe Scott. As she came back, she smiled at Linnell; and almost without discernible volition, Linnell began to move in her direction. Was Kathie working some malicious mental trick on my little cousin? But no. Kathie had no awareness of

Darkovan powers. I knew that. And nothing could get through that block I'd put on her.

Linnell touched Kathie's hand, almost shyly; in immediate response, Kathie put an arm around Linnell's waist, and they walked for a minute like that, enlaced. Then, with a sudden lithe movement Linnell drew herself, free and came and caught at me.

"There's Callina," I said.

The Keeper, aloof in her starry draperies, threaded her way through the maze of dancers. "Where have you been, Callina?" Linnell demanded. She looked at her sister's strange costume with sorrowful puzzlement, but she did not comment; and Callina made no attempt to justify or explain herself.

"Yes," I demanded, with an intent look at Callina, shading the words telepathically, "where *have* you been?"

She seemed unaware of either overtone, and her careless words were devoid of any hidden message that I could read. "Talking with Derik. He drew me apart to hear some long confused drunken tale of his, but he never did get it told. I don't envy you, darling," she added, smiling at her sister. "Fortunately all the wine conquered him at last—may he never be defeated by a worse enemy." She shrugged daintily. "Hastur is signaling to me. Beltran is there, I suppose it's time for the ceremony."

"Callina—" Linnell almost sobbed, but the woman moved away from her outstretched hands. "Don't pity me, Linnell," she said. "I won't have it." And I could tell that what she meant was, "I can't bear it."

I don't know what I might have said or done, but she drew herself away; her eyes brooded, blue ice like Ashara's, past me into silence. Bitterly helpless, I watched her shrouded form move through the bright crowd.

I should have guessed everything then, when she left us without a touch, silent and remote as Ashara's self, making a lonely island of her tragedy and cutting us all away from her. I listened, numbed, as Hastur made the formal announcement and locked the doubled marriage bracelets upon the arms of the pair. Callina was Beltran's consort from the moment Hastur released her hand.

I glanced round at Regis and suddenly, appalled, sucked in air; the boy had turned ashen gray. I slid an arm around him and half-carried him to the archway. He drew a sobbing breath as the cold air reached his face, and muttered, "Thanks. Guess you were right." And abruptly he doubled up and collapsed on the floor. His lax hand was clammy and his breathing was shallow. I looked around for help. Dio was crossing the floor, on Lerrys' arm—

Lerrys stopped dead in his tracks. He stared around wildly for a moment, his face convulsed; stiffened and clutched at Dio.

That was the first shock-wave. Then hell broke loose. Suddenly the room was a distorted nightmare, warped out of all perspective, and Dio's scream died in shivering air that would not carry sound. Then she was struggling in the grip of something that shook her like a kitten. She took one faltering step—

Then I saw two men standing together, the only calm figures in the distorted air. The harlequin and the horrible cowled man. Only now the cowl was flung back, and it was Dyan's cruel thin-lipped face that glared bleakly at Dio. She moved, fighting, another step, another; slid to the floor and lay there without moving.

I fought the paralysis of the warped space that held us in frozen stasis. Then harlequin and cowl turned—and caught Linnell between them.

They did not physically touch her. But she was in their grip as if they had bound her hand and foot. I think she screamed, but the very idea of sound had died. Linnell writhed, caught by some invisible force; a dark, flickering halo suddenly sprang up around them; Linnell sagged, held up hideously balanced on empty air; then fell, striking the floor with a crushing impact. I sobbed soundless curses; I could not move.

Kathie flung herself down by Linnell. I think she was the only person capable of free motion in the entire hall. As she caught Linnell in her arms, I saw for a moment that the tortured face had gone smooth and free of horror; a moment Linnell lay quiet, soothed, then she struggled in a bone-wrenching spasm and slackened—a loose, limp, small thing with her head lolling on her twin's breast.

And above them harlequin and cowled shadow swelled, took on height and power. For a moment, seeing clearly outside space, Kadarin's gaunt features blazed through the harlequin mask. Then the faces swam together, coalesced—and for a moment the beautiful, damnable face I had seen in Ashara's Tower reeled before my eyes; then the shadows closed down.

Only seconds later the lights blazed back; but the world had changed. I heard Kathie's scream, and heard the crowd milling and crying out as I elbowed and thrust my way savagely to Linnell.

She was lying, a tumbled, pathetic heap, across Kathie's knees. Behind her, only blackened and charred panels of wall and flooring showed where distortion and warp had faded to normal, and Kadarin and Dyan were gone—melted away, evaporated, not there.

I knelt beside Linnell. She was dead, of course. I knew that, even before I laid my hand to the stilled breasts. Callina thrust Kathie aside, and I stood back, giving my place to Hastur, and put an arm around Callina; but though she leaned heavily on me, she took no notice of my presence.

Around me I heard the stir of the crowd, sounds of command and entreaty, and that horrible curiosity of a crowd when tragedy strikes. Hastur said something, and the crowds began to thin out and clear away. I thought, *this is the first time in forty generations that Festival Night has been interrupted.*

Callina had not shed a tear. She was leaning on my arm, so numbed with shock that there was not even grief in her eyes; simply, she looked dazed. My main worry was now for her; to get her away from the inquisitive remnant of the crowd. It was strange I did not once think of Beltran, though the marriage bracelet about her arm lay cold against my wrist.

Her lips moved.

"So that was what Ashara intended..." she whispered.

With a long, deep sigh, she went limp on my arm.

CHAPTER TWELVE

The thin red sunlight of another dusk was filtering through the walls of my room when I woke; I lay still, wondering if the whole thing had been a delirious nightmare born of concussion. Then Andres came in, and the drawn face of the old Terran, grief deep in its ugliness, convinced me; it was all too real. I remembered nothing after Callina's collapse, but that wasn't surprising. I had been warned, after the head wound, not to exert myself; instead I'd been throwing myself into battle with some of the strongest forces on Darkover.

"Regis Hastur is here," Andres said. I tried to sit up; he pressed me flat with strong hands. "You young idiot, don't you know when you're done in? You'll be lucky to be on your feet again in a week!" Then his real feelings burst through the gruffness. "Boy, I've lost two of you! Don't send yourself after Marius and Linnell!"

I yielded and lay quiet. Regis came in, and Andres turned to go—then abruptly went to the window and jerked the curtains shut, cutting the lurid sunlight.

"The bloody sun!" he said, and it sounded like a curse. Then he went away.

Regis asked me gently, "How are you feeling?"

"How do you think?" My jaw set. "I have some killing to do."

"Less than you think, maybe." The boy's face was grim. "Two of the Ridenow brothers are dead. Lerrys will live, I think, but he won't be good for much, not for months."

I had expected that. The Ridenow were hypersensitive even to ordinary telepathic assault; he would probably lie in a semi-coma for months. He was fortunate to have survived at all. "Dio?"

"Stunned, but she's all right. Zandru's hells, Lew, if I'd only been stronger—"

I quieted him with a gesture. "Don't blame yourself. It's incredible that you're not completely burnt out; the Hasturs must be hardier than I ever thought. Callina?"

"Dazed. They took her to the Keeper's Tower."

"Tell me the rest. All at once, don't dribble out the bad news!"

"This may not be bad. Beltran's gone; he left the castle that night, as if all Zandru's scorpions were chasing after him. That leaves Callina free."

I felt sourly amused. Beltran could have stepped in, with the Comyn in disorder and shock, and seized the reins of power as Callina's consort. That had, no doubt, been the idea. But in Beltran of Aldaran—superstitious, Cahuenga of the Hellers—they had relied on the weakest of tools, and it had broken in their hand.

"This is bad. There are Terrans here, and they've put an embargo on the castle. And—" he stopped, but he was keeping something back.

"Derik—is he dead too?"

Regis shut his eyes. "I wish he was," he whispered, "*I wish he was.*"

I understood. Under terrible need, we had cut into Derik's mind. We could not have foreseen that greater forces would be loosed so soon after. Corus and Auster Ridenow were the fortunate ones; their bodies had died when their minds were stripped bare.

Derik Elhalyn lived. Hopelessly, permanently insane.

Outside I heard a strange voice, a Terran, protesting, "How the devil does one knock when there's no door?" Then the curtains parted and four men came into the room.

Two were strangers, in the uniform of Terran Spaceforce. One was Dan Lawton, Legate from Thendara.

The fourth was Rafe Scott, and he was wearing the uniform of the Terran service.

Regis rose and faced them angrily. "Lew Alton has been hurt! He's in no shape to be—interrogated—as you questioned my grandfather!"

"What do you want here?" I demanded.

"Only the answers to a few questions," said Lawton politely. "Young Hastur, we warned you before; stay in your own quarters. Kendricks, take the Hastur kid back to his grandfather, and see that he stays there."

The bigger of the Terrans put a hand on Regis' shoulder. "Come along, sonny," he said kindly.

Regis twisted away. "Hands off!" His hand, flashing to his boot, whipped out a narrow skean. He faced them across the naked steel, saying with soft, cold fury, "I will go when the *vai dom* Alton bids me—unless you think you can carry me out."

I said, "I prefer him to stay. And you won't get anywhere with violence in the Comyn Castle, Lawton."

He almost smiled. "I know," he said. "Perhaps I wanted them to see that. Captain Scott told me—"

Captain Scott.

"Traitor!" said Regis, and spat.

Lawton ignored that, looking down at me.

"Your mother was a Terran—"

"Black shame to me that I must admit it—yes!"

"Look," Lawton said quietly, "I don't like this any more than you do. I'm here on business; let me do it and get out. Your mother was—"

"Elaine Aldaran Montray."

"Then you are kin to— How well do you know Beltran of Aldaran?"

"I spent a year or so in the Hellers, mostly as his guest. Why?"

He countered with another question, this time to Rafe. "Exactly what relation are you two, anyhow?"

"On the Aldaran side, it's too complicated to explain," said Rafe, "Distant cousins. But he married my sister Marjorie. You could say—brother-in-law."

"No spy for Terra can claim kin here!" I sat up, my head exploding painfully, but too much at a disadvantage flat on my back. "The Comyn will look after the law in this zone. You go and attend to your affairs in the Terran Zone! Since that was your choice!"

"That is exactly what we're doing," Lawton said. Lerrys was working for us, so his brothers are our business; and they're dead."

"And Marius," said Rafe. "You never had a chance to hear it, Lew, but Marius had been working for Terra—"

I flung the lie into his face. "My brother never took a copper from Terra, and you know it! Lie to *them*, but don't try to lie to an Alton about his brother!"

"The plain truth will do," Lawton said. "You are right so far—your brother was not in our pay, nor a spy. But he worked for us, and he had applied for Empire citizenship. I sponsored him myself. He had as good a right to it as you, though you never chose to claim it. Even by your standards, that is no spy." Lawton paused. "He was probably the only man on Darkover working to bring about an honest alliance. The rest were out to line their pockets. How come this is news to you? You're a telepath."

I sighed. "If I had a *sekal* for every time I've explained that, I could buy and sell the Terran Zone," I said. "Telepathic contact is used to project conscious thoughts. Quicker than words, no semantic barriers—and no one but another telepath can listen in. But it takes deliberate effort: one to send, the other to receive. Then, even when I'm not trying, I get a sort of—well—leakage: I can feel; right now you're confused, and sore as hell about something. I don't know what and I'm not trying to find out; telepaths learn not to be curious. I've been in rapport with my brother. I know everything he knew. But I don't remember—and I don't want to remember."

Suddenly, from Lawton's complete calm, I knew he had simply been trying to goad me; to make me lose my temper and drop my barriers. He was half Comyn; for all I knew, he might be a telepath himself. He'd been trying to find something out, and whatever it was, he'd probably found it.

"I'll tell you why I'm here," Lawton said abruptly. "Usually we let city-states govern themselves, until the government collapses. It usually does, within a generation after the Empire comes. When we meet real tyranny, we depose it; planets like Darkover, we simply wait for them to fall apart. And they do."

"I heard it all on Terra. *Make the universe safe for democracy—and then for Terran Trade!*"

"Maybe," Lawton said, imperturbably. "While you rule peaceably, you can rule till the planet crumbles. But there's been disorder lately. Riots. Raiding. Smuggling. And too much telepathic dirty-work. Marius died after you had forced rapport on him."

Regis said, "Who told you those lies? I saw him die with a knife in his heart."

"Marius wasn't a citizen yet, so I can only ask questions about his death, not punish it," he said. "But there's another report that you're holding a Terran girl here, prisoner."

My heart pounded suddenly. *Kathie.* Had Callina and I rashly exposed this last secret of Darkovan science?

"The daughter of the Terran Legate on Samarra—Kathie Marshall. She was scheduled to leave Darkover on the *Southern Cross*, days ago; I thought she had gone. But she's missing, and someone saw her here."

Regis said indifferently. "There were a great many Terrans here Festival Night. Someone must have seen—" he raised his voice. "Andres? Bring the *comynara* here; she is with Dio Ridenow."

His eyes held an intensity whose meaning escaped me; I started to open my mind, but sensed his instant prohibition. Lawton and Rafe would both know it, if we were exchanging telepathic messages, even if they couldn't read what they were about.

Regis said, "I would not, of course, know anything about Miss—is it Marshall? But I know who you saw. The resemblance has caused us some amusement, and a little embarrassment. Since, of course, no *comynara* could possibly be permitted to behave in public as your *Terrananis* do."

Inward I raged and worried. What now? Why must they drag the name of the dead into this? After an eternity, I heard light, familiar footsteps, and Kathie Marshall came into the room.

She wore Darkovan dress; a ruffled gown that hung loose from her slender shoulders, her unbound hair dusted with metallic fragments. Bangles tinkled on her ankles and slender wrists.

"Kathie?" said Lawton.

Kathie raised a pretty, uncomprehending face. *"Chi'zei?"*

"Linnell, my dear," Regis drawled, "I have spoken of the foolish resemblance to some *Terranis;* I wished them to see at first hand."

I was praying that none of them knew Kathie well. The difference was so haunting that it struck me with passionate grief; a ghost, a mockery.

Kathie put a hand down to touch my face. It was not a Terran gesture. She walked and moved like a Darkovan. "Yes, Regis, I remember," she said, and I had all I could do to keep back a cry of astonishment. For Kathie was speaking the complicated, liquid-syllabled pure mountain Darkovan—not with her own harsh Terran accent but with soft quick fluency. "But should you have so many strangers around you when you are hurt? To tell you some fantastic story about the Terrans?"

It wasn't Linnell's intonation. But the fact remained, she was speaking Darkovan, and speaking it with an accent as good as my own or Dio's.

Lawton shook his head. "Fantastic," he muttered, "There certainly is a resemblance! But I happen to know Kathie couldn't speak the language anything like that!"

The big Terran broke in. "Dan, I tell you, I *saw*—"

"You were mistaken." Lawton was still looking intently at Kathie, but she did not move. Another false note. It is rudeness unspeakable to stare at an unmasked young girl on Darkover; men have been killed for it. Lawton knew it. Linnell would have been dying of confusion. But as that thought crossed my mind, Kathie blushed and ran out of the room.

"I'm trying to *tell* you," Kendricks said, "I was on spaceport duty when the Marshall girl left. I checked the passenger list after they were all drugged and tied-in. She certainly didn't get off after that, and it's been reported from Samarra by relay, so how could she be here? The fastest ship made takes seventeen days hyperdrive, between there and here."

Lawton muttered, "I guess we've made prime fools of ourselves. Alton, before I go, can you tell me how the Ridenow brothers died?"

Regis said, "I tried to explain—"

"But it didn't make sense. You said someone had a trap-matrix out. I know a little about matrices, but that's a new one on me."

No Terran can really grasp that concept, but I tried. "It's a sort of mechanical telepath that conjures up horrifying images from race-memory and superstition. The person who sets one can control the minds and emotions of others. The Ridenow are sensitives—disturbed mental atmospheres affect them physically. This one was so badly disturbed that it short-circuited all the neural patterns. They died of cerebral hemorrhage."

It was a grossly over-simplified explanation, but Lawton at least seemed to understand. "Yes, I've heard of things like that," he said, and I spied a strange, bitter look on his face. Then, to my surprise, he bowed.

"Thank you for your co-operation," he said. "There will be other matters to discuss when you are recovered."

Rafe Scott lingered when the others had gone.

"Look, if I could talk to you by yourself, Lew," he said, glowering at Regis.

Regis only said with angry contempt, "Get out of here, you filthy Terran half-caste!" He put his hand in the middle of Rafe's back, giving him a sharp push—more offensive than a blow.

Rafe turned around and hit him.

Regis' fist slammed into Rafe's chin. The Terran boy lowered his head, rushed in and clinched, and they swayed back and forth in a struggling, furious grip. All Regis' contempt, all the humiliation Rafe had suffered at the hands of the Comyn, exploded; they slammed at each other, the room filled with their pummeling violence. I lay there forgotten by both, yet somehow more a part of the fight than they were themselves. I felt, half deliriously, that the two halves of myself were slugging it out; the Darkovan Lew, the Terran. Rafe, once almost a brother—Regis, my best friend in the Comyn—both were myself and I was fighting myself, and each blow struck was in my own quarrel.

Andres settled it abruptly by collaring both the angry young men and jerking them violently through the curtains. "If you've got to fight," he growled, "do it outside!"

There was the brief sound of a scuffle, then Regis' voice clear and scathing. "I should dirty my hands!"

Somehow, being part of their contention, these words were strangely meaningful; as if my own inward struggle had been somehow resolved.

After a while Andres came in, keeping up a steady monotone grumble that was vaguely soothing. His hands were gentle as he looked at the half-healed wound at the back of my head; he ignored my profane protests that I was perfectly capable of taking care of myself, grinned when I swore at him, until finally I broke into rueful laughter that hurt my head, and let him do what he would. He washed my face as if I were a fretful child, would have fed me with a spoon if he'd thought for a minute that I'd allow it—I didn't—and finally dug out a pack of contraband cigarettes smuggled in from the Terran Zone. But when I had finally chased the old fussbudget off to rest, I could elude thought no longer.

Time had healed, a little, my grief for Marjorie. My father's death, bitterly as I regretted it, was more the Comyn's loss than mine. We had been close, especially toward the end, but I had resented the thing that made me half-caste. Much as I missed him, his death had set me at ease with my own blood. And the murder of Marius was a nightmare thing, mercifully unreal.

But Linnell's death was a grief from which I have never been free; that night my own pain was only an obligate to the torture of my nerves.

What had killed Linnell? No one had touched her, except Kathie. She was not, like Dio, a sensitive.

And then I understood.

I had killed Linnell.

All evening, intuitively, Linnell had been striving for contact with her duplicate. Their instinct had been better than my science. I—pitiful, damned, blind imbecile—I had blocked them away from one another. When the horror of Sharra had been loosed, Linnell had instinctively reached for the safety of contact with her duplicate. What had I said to Marius? *One body can't take it...*

And the bypass circuit in Kathie's mind had thrown Linnell into contact with me—and through me, into that deadly matrix in Kadarin's hands. Years ago, Sharra had been given a foothold in my brain. And force flows toward the weaker pole. It had all rushed into the unprotected Linnell, overloading her young nerves and immature body.

She had gone out like a burnt match.

Havoc had indeed raged in the Comyn. Linnell, the Ridenow, Derik, Dio. I smiled, grimly. The defenses I'd given Dio had probably saved her from the fate of her brothers. And after her malice—

Blinding light broke suddenly on me. There wasn't a scrap of malice in Dio. In her own way, the perverse little imp had been *warning* me!

A narrow chink of moonlight lay in a cold streak across my face; in the shadows there was a stir, a step and a whisper. "Lew, are you asleep?"

The dim light picked out a gleam of silvery hair, and Dio, like a pale ghost, looked down at me. She turned and slid the curtains back, letting the light flood the room and the moons peer over her shoulder.

The chill radiance cooled my hot face. I found no words to question her. I even thought, incuriously, that I might have fallen asleep and be dreaming she was here. I could see the shadow of the bruise lying on her cheek, and murmured, "I'm sorry I hurt you."

She only smiled, half-bewildered. Her voice was as dreamy as the unreal light when she bent down to me.

"Lew, your face is so hot—"

"And yours is so cool," I whispered. I touched the bruise with my good hand, wanting to kiss it. Her face was in shadow, very grave and still. Suddenly, forcefully, Callina came into my mind. Not the aloof Keeper, but the proud and passionate woman defying the council, refusing before Ashara to bare her mind to my touch—

Dio, too, had feared that. Could any woman endure that intimacy, that bond that was deeper than any physical touch? Callina, remote, precious, untouchable—and Dio, who had been everything to me that a woman can be to a man. Or almost everything. And why was I thinking of Callina, with Dio beside me? She seemed to be forcing the thought on me; so strongly, I was almost constrained to speak the name aloud. Her pallid face seemed to flicker, to be Callina's own, so dreamishly that I could not believe I was awake.

"Why are you here?"

Dio said, very simply, "I always know when you are in pain or suffering."

She drew my head to her breast. I lay there with my eyes closed. Her body was warm and cool at once and the scent of her was at once fresh and familiar, the mysterious salty smell of tears mingling with the honey and musk of her hair.

"Don't go away."

"No. Never."

"I love you," I whispered. "I love you."

For a moment Callina's sobs deepened—Callina? *Callina?* She was almost a physical presence between us; rather the two women blended and were one. To which one had I whispered my love? I did not know. But the soft arms around me were real.

I held her close, knowing with a sort of sick certainty that—as a woman—I had nothing for her now. The telepath's personal hell, just as painful as ever.

But it didn't seem to matter. And suddenly I knew that the Dio I had loved on Vainwal, passionate and superficial and hoydenish, was not the real girl at all. This was the real one. I was not the man she had known there, either.

I could not have spoken if I had tried. There was shame, and a proffered apology, in my kiss; but she gave it back as it was given, gently, without passion.

We fell asleep like little children, clasped in each other's arms.

CHAPTER THIRTEEN

When I woke, I was alone. For several minutes, in the morning sunlight, I wondered if the whole bizarre episode had been a dream; then, as the curtains parted and Dio came in, a grim smile turned up my mouth. In a dream, I would surely have possessed her.

"I've brought you another visitor," she said. I began to protest; I didn't want to see anyone. But she pulled the curtains aside—and Marja ran into the room.

She stopped, staring—then ran and flung herself on me with a smothering hug.

I loosened her, staring at Dio. "Gently, *chiya,* gently, you'll have me on the floor. Dio, how—"

"I learned about her when Hastur first brought her here," Dio said. "But Ashara's Tower is no place for her now. Take care of him, Marja *mea,*" she added, and before I could ask any more questions, she went away again.

Andres reported that there were Terrans still guarding the castle corridors, but no one came near us all day. I resigned myself to inaction, and spent the day playing with Marja and making a few hazy plans. She would not be taken from me again! Andres seemed puzzled, but there was no way to explain without speaking of Marjorie and Thyra, and even to Andres, I could not do that. I told him, simply, that she was my daughter; he gave me a knowing look and, to my relief, left it at that.

I tried to ask Marja a few careful questions, but the answers were vague and meaningless; all one could expect from so young a child. Toward nightfall, since no one had come to reclaim her, I told Andres to put her to bed in a sleeping-cubicle near my own, and when she had fallen asleep I left her there and called Andres.

"How many Terrans are in the castle?"

"Ten, maybe fifteen. Not Spaceforce—even Lawton wouldn't have that much insolence. They're in plain clothes, and they behave themselves."

I nodded. "None of them would know me by sight, I suppose. Hunt me up a suit of Terran clothes."

He gave me a bleak grin. "No use trying to stop you, I suppose. I'll look after the little lass, then. And, I don't have to be a telepath to know what you're thinking, *vai dom*. I've lived with your family half my life. If that don't answer your question, what would?"

There were many doors to the Alton suites, and the Terrans couldn't guard them all. In the hallways no one paid the slightest attention to me. They were looking after a Darkovan man with one hand; a man in Terran clothing, one hand stuck in a pocket, roused not the slightest curiosity.

I hesitated outside the Hastur apartments, wanting to take counsel with the old Regent; then, regretfully, passed. If he knew our plan, he might forbid me, and a thousand oaths bound me to obey him. Better not chance it.

I found Callina in her own rooms, seated before Linnell's harp; her head was buried in her arms and I thought she was crying; then with sudden suspicion, I grabbed her and jerked her head up.

She came up stiffly, resisting; her eyes, blank and dead, stared at me without recognition. "Callina!" I shouted, but I might as well have whispered. I dragged her bodily to her feet. Her eyes were fixed in a lifeless, blue-ice stare. "Wake up!" I shouted, and shook her hard. But I had to put her in a chair and slap her before the spark of life suddenly blazed in her eyes and her head went up.

"What do you think you are doing? Let me go!"

"Callina, you were in trance—"

"Oh, no! No!" She threw herself on me, pressing herself to me in desperate appeal. I caught the words, "Ashara" and "—send—her—out," but they meant nothing, and I held her away. I dared not touch her until this was over. Gradually, she calmed. "I'm sorry, Lew. I'm—*me* again."

"But who are you?" I said at hazard, "Dio? Ashara?"

She smiled, a sorrowful smile. "If you don't know, who does?"

I dared not show tenderness. "We've got to act tonight, Callina, while the Terrans think I'm still too weak to do anything. Where is Kathie?"

Her face twisted. "It's like Linnell's ghost—"

I dreaded it, too, but I said nothing, and finally Callina sighed. "Shall I go to her?"

"Let me," I said. I walked through two cubicles, finally found the one where we had taken Kathie. She was lying on a couch, almost naked, scanning a set of tiles; but she heard my step and started violently, catching a sort of veil around her. "Get *out!*" she squeaked. "Oh—it's you again!"

"Kathie, I haven't the slightest designs on you, except to ask you to dress and come with us. Can you ride?"

"Yes. Why?" She paused. "I think I know why. Something strange happened to me, I think, when Linnell was killed."

I couldn't discuss that. I reached to the dressing panel, rummaged among the forcebars and racks, finally pulled out some garments. I recognized them, with a stab of pain; Linnell's perfume hung about them; but there was nothing else I could do. I threw the armful in her lap. "Put these on," I said, and sank down to wait, but her angry stare made me recall, suddenly, the Terran taboos. I rose, actually reddening. How could Terran women be so immodest out of doors and so prudish within? "I forgot. Call me when you are ready."

A queer sound made me turn back. She was staring helplessly at the clothes.

"I've no idea how to get into these things!"

"After what you were just thinking at me," I said, "I'm certainly not going to offer to help you."

It was her turn to blush. "Besides—how can I ride in skirts?"

"Zandru, girl," I exploded, genuinely shocked now. "What else?"

"I've ridden all my life, but I never tried it in a skirt, and I'm not going to start. If you want me to ride anywhere, you can certainly get me some decent clothes."

"These clothes are perfectly decent."

"Damn it, get me some *indecent* ones then," she blazed. I laughed. I had to.

"I'll see what I can do, Kathie."

Fortunately, I knew where Dio slept, and no one stopped me. I parted the curtains and looked in. She was asleep, but sat up quickly, blinking. "Are things starting again?"

They had never stopped; we had simply been flung out of them. I explained what I wanted; she giggled, then the laughter broke off. "I know it isn't really funny, Lew. I just can't help it. All right, then. I think my things will fit Kathie."

"And can you find Regis, and tell him to slip out and find horses for us?"

She nodded. "I can come and go pretty much as I please. Most of the Terrans know me. Lerrys—" she stopped, biting her lip. There was nothing I could say; I'd hated her brothers and she knew it. Dio was as alone, now, as I was.

Seeing Dio made me remember something else. I slipped back to my rooms and got Rafe's pistol. There were still bullets in the chamber. I still abhorred these coward's weapons—but tonight I might be fighting men without honor or conscience.

When I went back to Kathie's rooms, Dio and Callina were already there, and the Terran girl had been dressed in the sleeveless tunic and close-fitting breeches which Dio had worn for riding on Vainwal. Callina, more conventionally dressed, looked on with mild disfavor.

"Fine, but how are we going to get out?"

I laughed. I was not Kennard Alton's son for nothing. The Altons, aeons ago, had designed the Comyn castle, and their knowledge was handed down, son to son. "Don't you know your own rooms, Callina?" I went into the central room of the suite, and stepped into certain imprints of the flooring. I cautioned them to stand back, then frowned; my father had told me of this doorway, but had never bothered to teach me the pattern; nor did I have a sounder to test the matrix lock. I tried two or three of the standard patterns, but they did not respond; then turned to Callina.

"Can you sound a fourth-level without equipment?"

Her face took on concentrated seriousness; after a minute a section of flooring dropped out of sight, revealing deep, dusty stairs that led away downward.

"Stay close to me," I warned, motioning them ahead. "I've never been down here before." Behind us the square of light revolved, spun—and we were in darkness.

"I wish that old great-grandfather of mine had provided a light! It's dark as Zandru's pockets!"

Callina raised her hand—and the tips began to glow. Light spread—sparkled—radiated from those twelve slender fingertips! "Don't touch me," she warned softly. The passage was long and dark, with steep steps, and in spite of the ghost-light dark and dangerous. Once Kathie slipped on the strangely slippery surfaces, and fell jarringly a step or two before I could catch her, and twice my outstretched hand broke sticky invisible webs. There was no rail, and I found it hard to balance, but Callina picked her way securely and delicately, never stumbling, as if the way were perfectly well known to her.

Down, and down. Finally a door slid back and we stood in the se-
mi-light of Thendara under three waning moons. I looked around. We
were in a disorderly section of the city where the Terrans probably never came twice in fifteen years. Down the dark street was a place where
horses were shod and swords and tools mended; here Regis was to meet
me if my message had reached him.

It had. He was there, standing in the shadow of several horses, in
the deserted street.

"Lew, take me with you? Leave the women here."

"We need Kathie. And someone has to stay here, Regis. This is
our only chance. If we don't make it, you'll have to make what terms
you can. I think, as a last resort, you might be able to trust Lawton."
I stopped, then shrugged, without finishing what I had started to say.
There was no point in farewells and we made none.

Out through the streets of Thendara; into the open country. We
passed a few houses and deserted farmsteads—they grew wider apart
and finally ceased. No one rode this path now; on the Forbidden Road,
radioactivity was still virulent in spots, from the Years of Desolation.
The road itself was safe now, but the fear lingered; too many men in
past days had died. Hairless, toothless, their blood turned to water because they had taken this path. The Comyn had fostered that fear with
tricks and traps; and now it was useful, because we could ride unseen.
Only Dyan knew those tricks and traps as well as I.

We skirted the site of the ancient spaceships, their huge bulk still
glowing feebly with the poisonous radiance. Then we were on the Forbidden Road itself; the canyon, nature's own roadway, which stretches
from the highest point in the Hellers down to the Sea of Dalereuth a
thousand miles away. Just wide enough for six horses to ride abreast,
thirty feet below the surface of the plain, and nearly a thousand miles
long, the Forbidden Road runs all across the continent as if some giant
or some God, in the lost years, had reached out and scratched the

molten land with a titan fingernail, cutting across mountains, foothills, plains.

Legend had it the Forbidden Road was the track where the Gods walked, ages ago, when they spread their terror on the land and the children of the Comyn were born with their minds awry with the strange Comyn Gifts. A barren land, seared of growth, the track of something that had marred the land to freakishness, creating the Comyn. Mutation? The children of Gods? I did not know or care.

Two of the moons had set, leaving a single pallid face on the horizon, when we turned aside from the Road and saw the *rhu fead*, a white, dim, gleaming pile, rising above the thinly gleaming shore of the lake of Hali. We reined in our horses near the brink. Mist curled up whitely along the shore, where the sparse pink grass thinned out on the rocks. I kicked a pebble loose and it dropped into the glimmering cloud-waves, sinking without a splash, slowly, visible for a long time. Kathie stared at the strangely-surfaced lake.

"That isn't water, is it?"

I shook my head. No living being, save those of Comyn blood, had ever set foot on the shores of Hali.

She said confusedly, "But I've been here before—"

"No. You have some of my memories, that's all." I patted her wrist clumsily, as if she were Linnell. "Don't be afraid."

Twin pillars rose white, a rainbow mist sparkling like a veil between them. I frowned at the trembling rainbow. "Even blocked, it would strip your mind. I'll have to do what I did before; hold your mind completely under mine." She shuddered, and I warned tonelessly, "I must. The veil is a force-field attuned to the Comyn brain. It won't hurt us but it would kill you."

She glanced at Callina. "Why not you?"

Callina shook her head. "It has something to do with polarity. I'm a Keeper. If I tried to submerge your mind for more than a second or two, it would destroy you—permanently." A curious horror showed in her mind. "Ashara showed me—once."

I picked Kathie up bodily. When she protested, I scowled. "You fainted once, and went into hysterics the second time I touched you," I reminded her grimly. "If you do that again, inside the Veil, I want to make sure you'll get out the other side."

This time, however, she was barriered against me, by my own bypass circuit. It was easy to damp out the alien brainwaves. We got through the shimmering, blinding rainbow, with blurred eyes; I set her down and withdrew as gently as I could.

The *rhu fead* stretched bare before us, dim and cool. There were doors and long passages, filled with chilly curls of mist. Kathie made a sudden turn into one passage and began to walk forward into the dimness.

"Lew, I know! How do I know where to go?"

The passage angled into an open space of white stone and curtained crimson. A dais, set back into the wall and paneled in iridescent webs, held a blue crystal coffer. I set my foot on the first step—

I could not pass. This was the inner barrier; the barrier no Comyn could penetrate. I leaned on an invisible wall; Callina, curious, put out her hands and saw them jerk back of themselves. Kathie asked, "Are you still blocking my mind?"

"A little."

"Then don't. That bit of you is what holds me back."

I nodded and withdrew the blocking circuit. Kathie smiled at me, less like Linnell than she had ever looked; then walked through the invisible barrier.

She disappeared into a blue of darkening cloud. A blaze of fire seared up; I wanted to shout at her not to be afraid, it was only an illusion—but even my voice would not pass the barrier reared against the Comyn. A dim silhouette, she vanished; the flames swallowed her.

Then a wild glare swept up to the roof and a burst of thunder rolled and rocked the floor.

Kathie darted back to us; and in her hand she held a sheathed sword.

CHAPTER FOURTEEN

So the Sword of Aldones was a real sword, after all; long and gleaming and deadly, and of so fine a temper that it made my own look like a child's leaden toy. In the hilt, through a thin layer of insulating silk, winking jewels gleamed blue.

It might have been a duplicate of the Sharra sword, but that now seemed an inferior forgery of the glorious thing I held.

This was not a concealment for a hidden matrix; rather it was a matrix. It seemed to have a life of its own. A tingle of power, not unpleasant, flowed up my arm. I gripped the hilt and drew it a little way—

"No," Callina said warningly, and gripped my hand. A moment, stubborn, I resisted; then slid it back into the sheath.

"That's that," I said harshly. "Let's get out of here."

Dawn was breaking over the lake when we came out, and the wet sunlight glinted, ominously, on steel. Kathie cried out, in terror, as three men stepped toward us.

Three men? No; two—and a woman. Kadarin, Dyan—and between them, slim and vital as a dark flame, Thyra Scott smiled up at me, her mocking mouth daring me to speak or strike. I caught the dagger from my belt. Thyra stood steady, her naked throat upturned to the steel.

My hand tilted and the knife fell from it.

"Get out of my way, witch!"

Her low, fey laughter raised a million ghosts, but her voice was steel. "What have you done with my daughter?"

"My daughter," I said. "She's safe. But you can't have her."

Dyan took a step, but Kadarin took his elbow and hauled him back. "Wait, you."

Thyra said, "We will bargain. Give me what the Keeper holds, and you go free."

"We will anyhow," I said.

Kadarin drew his sword. I should have known; it was the one bearing the Sharra matrix. "Will you?" he asked softly. "Better hand it over. I intend to kill you, but you couldn't give me a fair fight, not now." His eyes swept, with gentle contempt, from my bandaged head to my feet. "Don't try."

"I suppose you have Trailmen in hiding with your usual odds of twenty to one?"

Kadarin nodded. "They won't touch you. You're for me. But the women—"

"Go to hell," I snarled, and, flashing the sword from the sheath, I flung myself at Kadarin. The touch of the hilt poured that stream of overflowing life through me; the blood beat so hard in my temples that I was faint with it. Kadarin whipped up the Sharra sword. The swords touched—

The Sword of Aldones blazed blue fire! Like a living thing it leaped from my hand and clattered down, coruscating blue fire from hilt to point. The two swords lay crossed on the ground, streams of wild blue flame cascading about them. Kadarin was reeling.

I picked myself up. We stood back, neither daring to approach the fallen blades.

But Kathie darted between us and caught up both swords. To her, I think, they were only swords. She held one in either hand, carefully. The blue flames died.

"That won't help," Kadarin said, and added grimly, "Don't be a self-sacrificing fool. Give me the Sharra matrix and go. We couldn't take the

Sword of Aldones, maybe. But we can take the Sharra one, and we will. You could kill me, kill Dyan, kill Thyra—but you can't kill them all!"

Of course there was no choice. I had the women to guard. "Give it to him, Kathie," I said at last. This was only a draw. The real fight would come later.

"Give it up? Now?"

"I'm no hero," I said savagely, "and you've never seen the Trailmen fight." I took Sharra's matrix from her hand. Dyan stepped forward, but Kadarin elbowed him away. "Not you!"

It was fortunate we had Kadarin to deal with. When we fought, it would be to death—but it would be fair. "We can go. His word's good."

But Thyra flung herself forward, the knife bright in her hand. I twisted, just too late; she drove the knife into my side.

I got my arm up and knocked her hard, stunningly, across the face; then I sat down, hard, my hand to the numb slash. Blood dripped through my fingers. I heard Kadarin cry out like a berserker; dimly saw him shaking Thyra with maniac strength, back and forth, and finally he cast her to the ground, where she lay moaning. She had violated his word.

And then I blacked out.

THERE WAS A ROARING sound around me. I was lying with my head in Kathie's lap.

"Lie still. They're taking us to Thendara in a rocket-car."

"Keep him quiet, Kathie."

I reached for Callina's hand, but it was the cool brittle fingertips of Ashara that were fetters on my wrist, her cold eyes in the grayness. I jolted awake; something had touched my mind. Marja! I reached for her, but where she had been was only an empty place in the world—

I shook my brain free of delirium for a minute. Of course I could not touch Marja. Not in pain like this. I would not want to let her share this now.

But a man's mind is so alone, shut up inside the bones of the skull.

I sank into the gray night again.

I WAS WALKING....

There was an arm beneath my shoulders, and Kadarin's voice said, "Easy! He can walk. It's just a scratch, the knife turned on the ribs."

My eyes wouldn't focus. I heard someone say sharply, "Good God! Come in here and sit down."

The dizziness cleared. I was standing in the Terran HQ, a rolling view of the spaceport lying far below me, and straight before me, at a big glass-topped desk, Dan Lawton was standing, looking at me with surprise and concern. Kadarin's arm was still holding me upright. I pulled away; from somewhere out of my range of vision, Regis Hastur got up, came to me, took me firmly by the shoulders and put me into a chair.

"Who in the hell are you?"

Kadarin bowed, ever so slightly.

"Robert Raymon Kadarin, *z'par servu*. And you?"

Behind us, a door opened and Kathie's voice said anxiously, "Is he really—oh, hello, Dan."

The Terran Legate shook his head. "In a minute," he said to nobody in particular, "I shall begin to gibber. Hello, Kathie. It is you?"

She looked dubiously at me. "May I tell him?"

"Wait, wait. One thing at a time. I'll go nuts, if I have to unravel anything more just now. Kadarin. I've wanted to set eyes on you for quite a while. You know you've finally stepped over the line?"

"I claim immunity," Kadarin said harshly. "Lew Alton would have died at Hali. I had given him safe-conduct, and his life has been formally claimed; it is mine to dispose of as I will. I brought him here of my own free will, when I could have preserved my own immunity by staying away and letting him die. I claim immunity."

Lawton groaned. But Kadarin had the legal right of it. "All right. But no telepathic tricks."

He smiled bitterly. "I couldn't, if I would. Dyan Ardais ran off with the Sharra matrix. I'm as helpless as Lew, here!"

Rafe Scott came suddenly into the office. The boy's face took on a stunned look as he saw me, and Regis, and Kadarin, and Kathie; but he spoke to Lawton.

"Why have you locked Thyra up downstairs?"

"Do you know that woman?" Lawton demanded sharply.

"She's his sister," Kadarin said, while Rafe was still sputtering.

"Damn it!" Lawton exploded. "Every troublemaker on the planet is related to you one way or another, Rafe! She tried to murder Lew Alton, that's all. When we brought her in, all of a sudden we had a screeching maniac on our hands, so I had the doctor give her a shot, and dumped her in a cell to cool off."

Rafe came to me, his voice urgent. "Lew, why would Thyra—"

"Let him alone, you!" Regis shoved Rafe roughly away. I gripped Regis' arm. "Don't start another fight," I implored. "Don't! Don't!"

A moment he resisted, then shrugged, and sat on the arm of my chair, glaring at Rafe. "Wasn't Callina with you?"

"The medical officer kept her too," Kathie said. "She was dizzy—sick. She kept falling asleep."

Trance again? I sat upright, feeling lightheaded. "I've got to get to her!"

"You can't do anything now," Regis said.

"What are you doing here?"

Lawton answered for him. "I sent, last night, for the Regent, and we've been talking most of the night."

Regis said quietly, "We're finished, Lew. The Comyn will have to make terms. Even Grandfather realizes that. And if Sharra gets out of hand—"

The Sword of Aldones was lying across Lawton's desk; Kadarin came and stood over it. "I let Sharra loose," he said, "It was an experiment that misfired, that's all. But our damned idiot hero here made matters worse by taking the Sharra matrix off-world, and for six years, all those activated spots just ran wild. And now Dyan has it!" He turned restlessly, a prowling animal. "I knew Alton wouldn't deal with me on any terms. So I tried to find someone in the Comyn, anyone who would steal the thing back for me. Just so I could monitor those sites, and then destroy the matrix. But after all that work—" his shoulders sagged. "I walked from the trap to the cookpot, when I tried to deal with Dyan Ardais!"

"Did he kill Marius to get it?" Regis asked.

"I imagine so, I'm not sure, but I'm not very wise in the accomplices I choose, am I? That—" he pointed at the Sword of Aldones, "is a last resort. It will put Sharra out, permanently, but it's murder. Anyone who's ever been keyed into the Sharra matrix—"

Lawton said, "I'll keep it for the time being."

Kadarin laughed, a harsh animal sound. "Just try! Now that it's been crossed with Sharra's, even I—" he reached for the sword, then his hands contracted visibly, and he drew back with an audible gasp. Shaking his fingers, agonized, he glanced at Rafe and said, "You try."

"Not if I know it!" Rafe backed away.

Lawton was no coward. He reached over and took the hilt firmly. Then, in a shower of blue sparks, he went flying across the room. He crashed into the wall, fell, and picked himself up, dazed, rubbing his head. "Good lord!"

"My turn." I reached for the Sword, which had fallen to the floor. I managed to lift it to the desk, but finally, trembling, had to let it fall.

"I can touch it," I said, feeling the hot, unbearable tingling, "but I can't hang on to it."

"No one man can," Regis said. "But I'll keep it for the moment." Easily, he picked it up and belted it at his waist. "I am Hastur," he said quietly.

Then the Hastur Gift is the living matrix!

Regis nodded. The matrix had found its support and focus, the monitoring balance, in the brain and nerves of the Hastur who bore it. No one else could handle that sword—or even hold it without danger.

Sharra was only a dreadful and lethal copy of this.

"Yes," Kadarin said quietly. "I guessed. That was why your hand never healed, Lew. The wound itself was not so bad, but you'd handled the matrix, and human flesh and blood won't take it. I never did, without at least one other telepath in rapport—"

Suddenly, down the corridor, Thyra began to scream.

Kadarin jumped out of his chair. I sat bolt upright. That something which had set Thyra to mad shrieking had jolted in me, too; black emptiness, loss, tearing—

"Marja!" I almost sobbed the name.

Kadarin whirled to face me; I have never seen such a look on a human face, before or since. "Quick! Where is she?"

"What's the matter?" Lawton demanded.

Kadarin moved his lips, but no sound came. Finally he said, "Dyan Ardais has the matrix—"

I finished. "He doesn't dare use it alone. He saw me—what happened to my hand. He'll need a telepath, and Marja's an Alton—"

"Dirty, treacherous—" Kadarin's voice was thick with fear, but not for himself. My mind was open, and for a minute, seeing Kadarin, my hate receded. Regis turned, unbelted the Sword of Aldones, and put it into Kathie's hands. "Keep this," he said, "you're still immune. Don't be afraid; no Darkovan alive can take it from you, or harm you while you hold it." He turned to me, and without a word, knowing what he wanted, I gave him Rafe's pistol.

"What are you—"

Regis said tersely, cutting Lawton short, "This is a Comyn affair, and with the best will in the world, you could only hinder, not help. Rafe, come with me."

Kadarin said harshly, "You fool, it's for Marja! Go with him!"

They went. The rhythmic, hysterical shrieks never stopped. Kadarin stood still, as if holding himself in check with his whole body; then suddenly broke free. "I'm going," he shouted at Lawton over his shoulder, and slammed out of the room. Lawton grabbed my arm.

"No, you don't! Have sense, man! You can hardly stand on your feet!" He forced me into the chair again. "What set them off? Who or what is Marja?"

The screaming stopped, abruptly, as if a switch had been flipped, leaving a silence that was somehow frightening. Lawton swore and stamped out of the room, leaving me lying in the chair, swearing with helpless rage, unable to rise. I heard shouts and voices ringing in the corridors, and wondered what had happened now, and then Dio stormed into the room.

"And they left you here!" she raged. "What did that red-headed bitch do to you? And they've doped Callina—oh, Lew, Lew, your shirt's all blood—" She knelt by me, her face white as her dress. Lawton came stamping back and stood over me, his face furious.

"Gone! That Thyra woman is *gone*—out of a sheet-steel cell, with guards all over the place! When that happens, with a Comyn matrix mechanic in the building—" He caught sight of Dio and his scowl deepened. "I know you, you're that sister of Lerrys. What are you doing here?"

"At the moment," she blazed, "trying to see what's wrong with Lew—which nobody else is bothering about!"

"I'm all right," I muttered, angry at the solicitude which weakened me. But I let her take me down to the Medical Floor where a little fat man in a white coat grumbled about a damned uncivilized planet where he spent his time patching up knife wounds. He did me up in plastic shields which hurt like hell, burned me with ultra-light of some kind and made me swallow something red and sticky which burnt my mouth and made my head swim, but it took the pain away; and when the dizziness stopped, I could think clearly again.

"Where's Callina Aillard?"

"In there," Dr. Forth said. "Asleep. She was faint and sick, so I gave her a shot of hypnal and had a nurse put her to bed in the women's infirmary."

"Any chance she could be in shock-trance?"

He put the things he'd used under the light-machine. "I wouldn't know. She saw you stabbed, didn't she? Some women react that way."

I damned the man for a fool. Darkovan women don't faint at a little blood. What was he doing here, if he couldn't diagnose matrix-shock? And if he had drugged Callina, there wasn't a chance I could bring her out of it. Not until all the drug wore off.

"It might be best," Dio said quietly. "Before she wakes, I want to tell you all about Callina. Not now."

Lawton, in his office, was setting the mechanism of search into action. Time crawled by; I waited. Once his puzzlement exploded into frustrated questions. "Damn it, I still haven't figured out how the Marshall girl got here from Samarra. And I'm still trying to get it all straight—the way you, and Rafe, and this Thyra woman, and Kadarin, are all brothers and sisters or cousins or whatever. And now this Thyra person vanishes into thin air! Did you witch her out of there some way?"

"I did not." Thyra could lie in a cell forever, for all I cared.

As the narcotic slowly wore off, I felt pain in my side again, but deeper down was that horrible sense of something torn away—I was afraid to know what it was.

The bloody sun of Darkover had reached its height and begun to angle sharply downward when I heard dragging footsteps and Regis and Rafe and Kadarin came in.

Regis had changed shockingly in a few hours. There was blood on his face, and blood on his sleeve, but it went deeper than his first serious fight. The last trace of the boy had burnt away and it was a man, and a Hastur, who looked at me in despair.

"You're hurt!" Lawton exclaimed, with the horror of a Terran for personally inflicted wounds.

"Not much. Cut my shirt up, mostly. I fought with Dyan."

"Dead?" I asked.

"No, damn it!"

Lawton demanded, "Kadarin, where's that woman of yours?"

Kadarin's gaunt face contracted in fear. "Thyra? Isn't she here with you? Zandru's hells, how can I tell her—" He covered his face with his hands. Suddenly he came to me. All the rest of the people in the office might as well have been on another planet for all the regard he gave them, and he looked into my eyes with an intensity that burned years away; back to the days when we had been friends, not sworn foes.

My voice came through dry lips.

"Bob, what is it? What's happened?"

His face twisted. "Dyan! Zandru send him scorpion whips! Naotalba twist his feet off in hell forever! He's taken her into Sharra—my little Marguerhia." His voice broke. The words burned at me like acid. Dyan, with the Sharra matrix. Marja, a child but an Alton—a telepath. And the blankness where she had been, the sense of something torn away.

Then she was dead.

Marjorie. Marius. Linnell.

Now Marja.

Lawton did not press us for details. He must have known we were all touching our last reserves of strength. I found myself sitting and asking questions as if anything could matter now. "Andres?"

"Dyan left him for dead, but he may pull through."

It was savage comfort to know that Andres had defended her like that. "Ashara?"

Dio stood up, her mouth pinched tight. I think we had all forgotten she was there. "Regis! Keep them! I am going to the Tower!"

I cried, "What for?" but she was already gone.

Lawton said grimly, "The first thing is to have Dyan picked up. If he has the little girl—"

Kadarin broke in. "You can't! There's no way to take the Sharra matrix away from him now. I've had the thing in my own hands often enough to know! Dyan could get it away from Marius only because he didn't know how to guard himself. No man living—" Kadarin started upright. "Lawton! All of you! Bear witness! His life is mine, when, how and as I can kill him, fair fight or unfair, his life is—"

"Mine!" I cut through his words. "Marja was mine! And whoever kills him, owes me a life—"

"You pair of maniacs!" Lawton said. "Let's catch him first, before you start fighting for the privilege of killing him!"

With a gesture that was animal in its ferocity, Kadarin said, "If he frees Sharra, don't trust *me!* I'm the master-seal and I'll be right *in* it!"

Regis turned to me. "Well, Lew, it will have to be you. You've touched Sharra, but you're sealed to the Comyn too. If we could hold you in rapport from *here*, you could go into the Sharra matrix—"

I cracked, then. "No!" I shouted. "No!" They could all die before they'd force me into that; why should I care now if Sharra ravaged Darkover? What had I left to lose? I grabbed the pistol out of Regis' belt, and snapped off the safety. "I'll blow out my own brains first!"

Regis' hand caught mine in a bone-crushing grip. We struggled briefly, crazily, but he had two hands; the recoil of the gun knocked me back and the bullet fired harmlessly through the window, in a burst of shattering glass. Regis shook my cramped fingers from the butt.

"You're insane!" he said. He tossed the pistol to Rafe. "Here. This was yours originally, wasn't it? Take it. It's been around a lot lately; One lunatic is enough!"

Lawton swore, kicking at the glass on the floor. "I ought to throw you all in the clink. Rafe, go get somebody to clean this mess up, and take Alton downstairs. He's off his head again."

I dragged to my feet, but I had to hold the chair. "I'm a prisoner?"

"Hell, no! But you walk out of here now, you'll pass out on the sidewalk! Man, use your head! Go on down to the infirmary! We'll let you know when we need you!"

Quite suddenly the rage dissolved, leaving me empty and numb. Kadarin unfolded his long legs and came to me. "Truce, Lew," he said quietly. "Marja was mine, too. We can't do much now. You're worn out. Maybe later we can figure out some way to get me out of that hellish thing before Dyan burns us all to hell-and-gone." His eyes met mine; there was no hate left in them. Mine, too, had burnt away.

I stumbled and let myself lean wearily on his arm. "Truce," I said.

So it was Kadarin who took me down to Medical and into the hospital wing. I sat down on the cot in the cubicle, my emotions burned out but my nerves jumping and my telepathic barriers nonexistent. I bent wearily to pull off my boots.

"Need any help?"

I asked him, straight, "You think Dyan will let Sharra loose?"

"I'm damn sure he'll try."

It felt unreal. For six years my main compulsion had been to kill Kadarin. I had pictured it to myself a thousand times, and here we were, talking, quietly and rationally and from the same side. It felt unpleasant, but somehow sensible. I supposed it was the Terran way of doing things.

"Want me to get you something from the medic?"

"No." I added, grudgingly, "No, thanks."

Then I looked up, squarely at him. I knew he would never stoop to lie about it. "Bob, was it by your order that Marjorie was—forced into the Sharra fire, that last time? Was it your way of revenging yourself on me? When you knew—" I swallowed, "that it would kill her?"

"Why would I kill *her*—to revenge myself on *you*?" He flung the question at me with a passionate sincerity I could not doubt; the same agonized question that had been tormenting me for six years.

"Lew, I knew Sharra as no living man has ever known. There was no danger, not for either of the girls, while I was in control. You know I loved Thyra, yet I managed to keep her safe." His face was bitter, agonized. "There aren't ten men alive who can determine the limits of safety for a woman they've had, but I did it for Thyra! Marjorie—"

His dark face was ravaged by such misery that I almost pitied him; his barriers were down too, and the violence of his grief was like a burning in me. He would never be free of that grief, that guilt. "Marjorie—Margie was just a child, I thought. She never told me! I swear I never knew you had been her lover! I swear it!"

I rolled over and buried my face, unable to endure it, but Kadarin went on, his voice heavy with pain. "So she went into it—and you know what happened. Any woman would have died coming from the arms of a lover to the pole of such power, and I've hated you for that—"

His voice suddenly softened into deep compassion.

"But it never occurred to me that you couldn't know. Hell, you were just a kid yourself. A pair of babies, you and Marjorie, and I never even warned you. Zandru's hells, Lew, talk about revenge, you had yours!"

Abruptly he was calm; dead calm. He said without inflection, "I claimed your life once. I give it back to you."

I looked up at him, equally numbed. He had claimed my life; a solemn obligation, irrevocable in Darkovan law, while we both lived. Had another killed me, he would have been legally obligated to track down and kill my murderer. But Darkovan law was collapsing around us. We stood in the smashing rubble. I did not know my own voice when I said, "I'll take it from you."

Gravely, unsmiling, we shook hands.

"Tell me this," I said wearily. "Why was Thyra's child mine?"

There was irony in his gaunt face. "I thought you'd have that all figured out. I hoped for a telepath son, with the Alton Gift."

Damned, insolent—

He said evenly, "Thyra never forgave me. I was so pleased with Marja that she was jealous, she refused to have the child where I could see her—" Suddenly his face twisted again. "It will kill Thyra! I swore Marja should not be used as a pawn, and I couldn't even keep her safe. Thyra has pretended so long to hate the child. Gods! Great Gods! Everything I love, everyone I love, I hurt or kill!" I flinched with the anguish of his despair. Abruptly he turned and went out, slamming the door so violently that the walls trembled.

CHAPTER FIFTEEN

I must have slept.

I opened my eyes at last in the bare infirmary cubicle to see Callina kneeling beside me. Her soft eyes were filled with tears; she seized my hand, but did not speak. I wanted to catch her in my arms and crush her to me; but Kadarin's words still held me, compelled with horror. For her very life, I dared not touch her.

But it would be harder than ever; I sensed, without knowing how, that some inner reserve in Callina was gone. There was no longer that chill, that conscious and wary aloofness.

"We've gone through it all for nothing, Callina," I said. "Marius and Linnell are gone, we've let the Comyn have our lives to play with, and what have we got?"

"There may still be something to save. Darkover—"

"The hell with Darkover! Let the Terrans have it and welcome!"

Callina passed her hand briefly across my eyes. I saw, in a blur, the horrifying face I had seen once before. It vanished; I saw Dyan, and Kadarin.

"The Sword of Aldones will cancel out Sharra," she said. "Kadarin was helping them to make plans, when he—vanished. He just wasn't there! Like Thyra."

That meant Sharra was free. I looked helplessly at the girl. "I've tried," I told her, "but I can't even touch the Sword of Aldones. Regis can, but he can't use it alone. No one man can."

Her fingers closed blindly on my good hand. "Ashara said you could use me for a focus—"

I shook my head. I couldn't hurt Callina that way. I would literally have to tear our two minds to pieces and rebuild them into one. I'd been through it myself, I could take it. But Callina!

Her voice was soft and resolute. "It's— well, it's you. And I want to."

Her bravery shamed me. Whatever happened, no woman should outdo me in courage. Suddenly, tenderly, I gave her arm a little shake. "All right, girl," I said, "we'll try it. But think about it. I want you to be sure."

"I'm sure now," she said.

It was strange to see her there; lovely Callina, all the beauty and mystery of the *comynari,* star-like and remote, there in that bare white cubicle. The note of grotesquerie in these surroundings, the tumbled cot where I had slept, made it all seem more, not less, strange.

She laughed, nervously; her hand in mine felt cold and fragile. Physical contact can lay the mind bare. I would have liked to hold her in my arms for this, but I did not dare. I had learned with Dio how such contact can break down barriers, but I forced the thought back. I felt curiously shy; I did not want to touch Callina's mind with another woman in the forefront of my thoughts.

I reached for contact.

For a moment there was a frighteningly familiar resistance; like Dio, every defense of her mind went up to bar me away. This time I made it a rough shock-wave; her hand tore loose from mine and she slumped down, her arms over her head as if by this desperate hiding she could arrest the soul-stripping contact. She did not resist actively, but her passive, trembling terror was worse. It was worse than anything I had ever had to do.

A tense moment of shock, and then Callina, white and shaking, snapped the rapport, sobbing wildly. I let it break and drew her into my arms, and gradually the weeping quieted. "I— I tried so hard—"

"I know." She had made every effort to endure the unbearable. Perhaps no woman can endure that absolute rapport with a man. If I had kept on, forced the resistance—it hadn't killed Marius, and Callina was Keeper, a *comynara*—but I simply was not capable of torturing a woman like that. It was worse than rape.

There was an alternative. It was drastic, but I was desperate. "Could you make the rapport?" I asked her. I said it easily, but inside, I was shaking. It put me wholly at her mercy; although a Keeper, she was not trained in handling that particular kind of focus.

Could I endure the forcible breaking of all my barriers?

I had closed off those old areas, years ago, to save my sanity.

I dropped that line of thought. I had to endure it, simply because I was stronger than she. Her touch was uncertain, fumbling, raw—an agony. It was desperately hard to keep from flinging her out of my brain; but with grim self-command, I endured it, lowering each barrier as she touched it. *How had she come to be Keeper, if she was as clumsy a telepath as this?* The bridge was stronger now, but she had not made the decisive move that would snap identity and bring it to completion; and I dared not move.

But it was so close to complete that I grew tense with the unbearable need to have it done, even if it killed us both. Force flows toward the weaker pole. I, who had chosen the passive part, was overloaded to the limit of endurance. I could neither see nor hear her now. If I made a move to end the torture, I could burn us both out. But if this did not end soon, I must risk it, even to the release of death.

Then the shock, the numbing flare of contact—

Regis!

Unbelievably, for a single unendurable moment, we—I—it *fused* into an impossible *triple* rapport. The load of emotion was terrible, breaking down every barrier in each brain, and our three minds went into one great glare of force, too vast and too searingly painful to comprehend.

Groping for sanity, I forced the rapport apart. We were three separate people again. Then, as blinding physical pain forced itself on me, Regis was incredibly there in the room with us, and he caught me as I pitched forward in a dead faint.

"DAMN IT, THIS IS GETTING to be a habit," I said shakily. I was lying on the bed again, Regis and Callina looking down at me anxiously. Regis pressed my hand as I sat up. "You've been doing all the hard work," he said.

"What happened?"

"Don't you know? How did I get here, anyway?" He swallowed convulsively and turned to Callina. Although we were deep in rapport, our conscious thoughts had dropped apart and I could not tell what they were thinking. But three! Even the Altons could link only two, and that with infinite danger! THREE!

Regis said, "What happened to us? I only know that something exploded in me—then it broke up, and I thought you were dead, Lew. I couldn't think of anything but to get to you and Dio. I didn't even know where you were, I was frantic, then all of a sudden I was here, and you pitched off the bed, and I grabbed you," he finished blankly.

"Callina and I had tried to link minds in focus—"

"Callina?" Regis stared. Callina suddenly stood on tiptoe and put her lips lightly against his. "Regis," she said softly, "we aren't resentful. We can—make room for you."

Regis put his arms around the girl and held her. "Doesn't he know? Not even now?"

"I've always been barricaded," she said.

Regis let her go, turning abruptly to me. "Now that we're aware, and guarded, let's set up contact again and see what this thing is, and what kind of power we have with it. As far as I know, this is something pretty new, and almost unique."

Callina reached out and made the linkage; this time there was no hesitation or fumbling, and I glanced at her with a surge of possessive pride. Regis, rather red about the ears, looked round.

If you two are going to think things like that at each other, his thought twisted humorously into ours, *I'd better drop out!*

Then the circle of contact was complete. Yet, strangely, the personal barriers were back, intact. We could work as one, at the deep levels; but identity remained inviolate, and privacy. We were three separate personalities; only for the first fusion was there that tearing down of emotions, of barricades.

Yet there was a sympathy, a togetherness that was extremely pleasant. It was as if all my life I had been getting along with a third of my brain.

Three telepaths, though not in rapport, had been needed to handle the Sharra matrix. This deep linkage, made through the living matrix of Aldones, was our weapon. Regis was the sword blade. Mine was the strength behind the sword; the Alton Gift, that hyper-developed psychokinetic nerve, was the hand to direct that striking force. And Callina, locked between hand and blade, was the sword hilt; the necessary insulation.

Yes, there was symbolism in concealing these things in a sword. Regis and I, Hastur and Alton—sword and hand—could never join power to strength, without exhaustion, nerve depletion and death—unless Callina were between us. The explanation swam up from somewhere in our linked minds. Comyn race-memory, perhaps, for they were not conscious memories. And Regis himself was the focus, the energy-source, the matrix if you will, through which, by means of the talisman sword, we could tap the energy-source and power of Aldones. Son of Hastur who was the son of Light—we stood close to what my race called a God.

My acquired knowledge knew this was a rational thing, science, mechanical and explainable; but there was a residue I could not explain. The *feel* of an actual living entity behind the Sword obsessed me.

I had felt the daemon-touch of Sharra. This was not evil—and somehow, that frightened me more. Infinite good is as terrifying as infinite evil.

But I was still physically weak, and Regis (*Guard your strength, Lew, you will need it soon!*) dissolved the linkage. I almost regretted it; a man's mind is a fearfully lonely place. Yet I could not have borne much more.

Regis touched Callina's arm. "Don't wait too long," he warned, and went away.

I feared that she, too, would withdraw; but, still tentative, she remained in contact, an immeasurable comfort. Her fingers laced in mine; closer yet was the delicate caress of her thoughts, and as I lay there, my face resting against her knees, I felt again a familiar, cool sweetness. The women tangled again in my thoughts, like the prism facets of a jewel.

How long the interval lasted I have no idea, but with a suddenness terrific in its impact, we both felt Regis, a desperate clamor in our minds, and knew that he had unsheathed the Sword.

And even as that warning rang out, space reeled, and we were flung together into the great courtyard of the Comyn Castle. Before us Regis stood, braced and erect, and in his hand the Sword of Aldones—live, shimmering blue from hilt to point. I caught my breath, and Callina cried out, a strange wordless cry; then she reached out, drew our three hands together on the sword-hilt and we were ONE.

Through my suddenly-extended senses, I made out, at the far end of the court, a wavering black mist through which pulsed strange flame. Sharra's fires! Hell-fires! I sensed, rather than saw, the other triad there.

Kadarin, Thyra, and Dyan Ardais.

The sight maddened me. For an instant I was one person again, and I leaped at Dyan, pulling out of the linkage. But as I touched him the blue lightning exploded, and we were flung apart; for Kadarin faced Regis, the Sharra sword naked in his hands.

But this time the swords did not short-circuit in flames. I was aware of a luminous mist that surged from the Sword of Aldones; it wrapped Regis in a rainbow aurora, glowed like a cape around Callina's shoulders, folded me in lucent brilliance. It licked out at the darkness that was Sharra. And in that dark center, like figures of smoke, Kadarin and Dyan and Thyra pulsed with the beating heart of the Thing they had evoked.

Darkness, comet-shot with the lightning that flared from the matrix-swords, crossing and re-crossing. It was not Regis and Kadarin fighting with identically forged swords. It was not even matrix warring against space-twisting matrix, or linked minds against linked minds. No. Something tangible and alive and intelligent fought behind them. Regis and Kadarin were only the poles of their power. The real forces were not warring in this world at all, or the planet would have been torn from its orbit and sent reeling through the dark night of space forever.

But enough projected here to be dangerous. Kadarin, beaten back, snatched hastily at his belt; with a quick, deadly flick, his knife flashed, and I was so much a part of Regis that for a moment I did not know whether it had struck him or myself. Only the deadly searing pain in my heart, and I felt, not saw, the Sword of Aldones drop from a limp hand. Regis slipped to the paving-stones. But he was still part of the linkage; as Kadarin drew himself upright, I lunged to grip the Sword of Aldones. Using it—only as a sword now—I drove the point through Kadarin's heart. He fell without a cry. Sharra's matrix-sword clattered on the pavement. I wrenched the Sword of Aldones free. It was over.

The luminous haze coiled up; the black mist pulsed and weakened, linkages broken. Then, abruptly, I leaped back, for Regis was incredibly on his feet again. He caught the Sword of Aldones from my hand. There was a stain of blood on his shirt, but he seemed unwounded; untouched. The threefold linkage snapped together again. Behind us, Callina stood, blazing at Thyra with a strange terrible intense stare. Thyra, too, stood locked, intent, motionless. None of us had uttered a single sound since the cry that had announced our coming.

A slim, girlish form burst suddenly from an opened door and ran madly, as if compelled, toward Dyan. Kathie! A few inches short of where he stood, she stopped, digging in her heels in panic terror; but Dyan caught her about the waist with one arm and snatched up the Sharra-sword. Kathie screamed. She had been immune; but now, my block withdrawn from her mind, her blindness to Darkovan forces was withdrawn. Linnell's duplicate—with Linnell's powers. Dyan forced her savagely into the Sharra triad. Kathie and Dyan and Thyra seemed almost to coalesce, to flow together.

The Sword of Aldones stirred like a live thing. Then Callina flung up her free arm and with all the concentrated force of a Comyn Keeper, wrenched Thyra out of the Sharra triad. It was only telepathic contact; not our deeply-molded rapport. I saw the lightning blast over Dyan, beat at him, and Callina's cry rang in my brain.

"Now, Lew! Now!"

Desperately, a bare chance, I forced a wedge between Dyan and his pawn. Kadarin had been taken so far into Sharra that he could not withdraw. Hate Dyan as he would and did, they were sealed together. But Thyra might be still vulnerable. I sent, frantically, one thought to Thyra.

Marja! Marja is dead! Dyan killed her!

Thyra moved like a striking snake. She wrenched the Sharra matrix from Dyan's hand; and with all the fury and rage and concentrated power of a mind trained by Kadarin, turned on him. And all the concentrated force of my Alton Gift struck through her as I, once sealed to Sharra, turned that full force-flow on Dyan.

And I saw Dyan crumple, shrivel and fall to the pavement, his mind thinned and gone. Stone dead.

The black mist pulsed like a heartbeat. It was trying to draw me into it! For a moment Regis and Kathie were flung out of the triads and for a moment it was threefold; Thyra, in Sharra; Callina, in Aldones; and I, pole of power, caught between them in that terrible struggle.

But our threefold linkage was stronger; the link broke and I was free of Thyra—and Sharra. In the storms of living light Callina and I moved close, Callina's hand insulating Regis' hand from mine on sword hilt, her mind guarding us one from the other. If Regis and I had directly touched minds, if we had even physically touched hands, the power would have seared us to cinders.

The pulsing black mist swept back, gathering itself for fresh assault, coagulating around Thyra and the dead men.

And Kadarin rose!

He was dead. He must have been dead. Yet horribly, with the galvanic movements of a strung puppet, he rose. I saw the blackness shake itself as three hands met on Sharra's hilt. Fire-colors gleamed in its depth, and there was a tall shining in the black mist, that swept on us. The three shadows twisted like smoke. Then, through the darkness, the face looked out. The face I had seen on the black night when terror walked in the Comyn and Linnell died.

But this time I knew what it was.

Long before Ashara, the Keeper, a further Keeper—a woman, born a Hastur, with the living matrix inherent in body and brain—had forged a matrix which should duplicate the powers of the Sword of Aldones. Two identical matrices cannot exist in one space and one time; and Sharra, Keeper of the Hasturs, had thrust herself outside *this* world.

Yet the matrix, not the living matrix of her brain, but the talisman matrix of the Sharra sword, remained here; and gave her a foothold in this world, through which she could be summoned when telepaths of certain skill should call her forth. Changed as she was, she still had power. And they called her daemon, Goddess.

But Sharra had been bound once, by the Son of Hastur. So ran the legend Ashara had repeated. Now another Son of Hastur, braced to endure the force by a rapport of three Comyn minds, held the Aldones matrix, intent on forcing her back again.

And under that power, space twisted and opened worlds reeled; Kathie was thrust back first, through the interlocking universes, to her own place from which we had snatched her. And in one thing, at least, the balance was restored.

Now Thyra and Kadarin, alone, together, held that focus of Sharra's power. They called me to them! I, once sealed to Sharra, wavered and bent like a candle in the wind toward that monstrous thing I had helped, years ago, to summon. I caught desperately at Callina to steady my hold.

Callina faltered. The strength of Aldones' power ceased; again the confusion, while lightnings danced at the heart of the black flame where the Face of Sharra stared out horribly and beautifully between the reeling worlds.

Callina was—GONE!

Only Ashara's cold, only Ashara's icy nothingness, thinned against the eternities of space. I felt the triad of Aldones dissolve. Despairing, I felt myself drawn toward the ravenous maw of Sharra....

Then, between a breath and a breath, there was a sharp shattering, as if a crystal broke under a cruel touch, and Callina was there again; I felt her strength, freed, cool and delicate, locking me to Regis again. Held steady. The blue lightning surged up, and our tripled brain was forged, suddenly, and welded, into a Cup. And into the Cup of Power flowed a force and a glory.

Regis seemed to grow taller, to take on height and majesty, and the cloak of blue light lapped his limbs.

And clothed in his cloak of living light Aldones came!

Like a white spark I could see the Sharra matrix, blazing out through the metal of the sword that held it. Pointing straight at the coruscating light that circled Regis like a diadem.

Once, I think, Kadarin might have held Sharra's power completely, and conquered. Nerves and body and brain—it was hardly sure at the last which was man, which matrix. But Kadarin was human; and at the end, when his sustaining hate of me had faded, I think there was something in him which broke and played traitor; which made him will for self-destruction; which broke Sharra and made the Thing vulnerable.

Two identical matrices cannot exist in one space. While separate brains controlled them, they were non-identical enough to remain, though the stress-conditions put the ground of battle in a little place outside space and time. But Sharra's instrument had broken first. I knew, because for a moment everything that was weak or evil in me fought with Sharra, and for a moment, at the end, I was one with Kadarin and Thyra again, back in the old days. All the immense strength and courage of Kadarin, all Thyra's beauty, generosity, grace, before the alien horror strangled her womanhood, these fought for Sharra too.

Then the face dimmed to a wraith; Kadarin and Thyra, two tiny, separating ghosts, were flung into each other's arms, and for a moment I saw them clinging together, silhouetted against the dissolving mist and fires. Then they were swept away, as Sharra's ghost-face vanished into some reeling hell of darkness, and with it went Thyra and Kadarin, somewhere, somewhere....

Aldones! Lord of the Singing Light! Is there mercy for them, too?

Then that, too, was gone, and I, Lew Alton, was kneeling in the damp dawnlit courtyard, arms around Callina, before a shaking, trembling boy holding a sword from which all the lights had faded. And there was no sign of Kadarin or of Thyra or of Kathie. Dyan lay dead, a blackened corpse, on the scorched paving-stones. And in his hand the Sharra sword lay broken, a few shattered pieces of metal. There was no matrix now in the hilt of the sword. The hilt, blackened with fire, was dull and grayed, and the jewels lay scattered on the stones. The first rays of the red sun touched the castle turrets, and seemed to tremble for a moment in the heart of the jewels.

They shimmered, evaporated like bright spots of blue dew—and were gone. The sword of Sharra was broken—and the power of Sharra was broken in this world, forever.

Regis still held the Sword of Aldones. He was white, and trembling as if with deadly cold. Then, slowly, he sheathed the Sword. A flowing peace seemed to radiate from him, enlacing us in its net. The Sharra matrix had made Kadarin, who was not a bad man or a weak one, into a fiend. The Sword of Aldones had made Regis—what?

"Regis—" My lips were stiff on the sound of his name, "What are you?"

"Hastur," he said gravely.

But the legend said Sharra was bound in chains by the son of Hastur, who was the son of Aldones, who was the son of Light.

He turned away and walked toward the archway. His face was the face of a God, at that moment, yet something less—and more. Supreme content ... and awful loneliness. Then that, too, dimmed out, and it was only a grave young man's face, the face of one doomed to walk forever with the memory of an hour's godhead—and be forevermore denied it.

The rising sun touched his hair, snow white.

He disappeared through the arched door.

And I saw Dio Ridenow walking from the Keeper's Tower, slowly, dazed, like a woman in a dream. Now when it was over—but I had no thoughts for Dio, for Callina had risen, and drew me to my feet.

And for the first time without fear, I took Callina in my arms, crushing my mouth to hers.

And all desire died as I looked into the cold eyes of Ashara.

I should have known, all along.

CHAPTER SIXTEEN

Only a moment and it was Callina again, clinging to me, crying; but I had seen, and I knew. My arm fell and I stared in horror as she turned away, desolately. "Sharra," I heard her whisper, "Sharra... Then it was no use, no use for me, and I cannot live...."

"Not by treachery, Ashara!" Dio faced the sorceress steadily. "Not by damning another as you doomed Callina! You failed, because Lew was too human, and because Callina was not human enough! You failed, you failed!"

Stricken, madness rocking my brain, I came to where the frail figure cowered before Dio. Callina, Ashara—I could not tell. They blended; were one. Reason swam away; I took Callina blindly in my arms and the form and the face shifted and changed and were now Callina and now Ashara and now Callina again; then a look of peace and my arms were empty, and a whisper faded and died and was still.

"Dio!" I sobbed the name and went to her arms like a hurt child, "Dio, Dio, have I gone mad?"

There were tears on Dio's face. "I tried so many times to tell you. Ashara was not real, had not been real for generations. Didn't you wonder why her Tower room seemed so immense? It was not in the Tower at all, the blue door was a matrix, a— a gateway to somewhere else. She was only a— a thought-form by now. She lived *in* the matrix, and whenever she left it, to take place in Comyn Council, she went in the body of one of the Keepers. Her power was so immense, and they were so frail, that for many generations she effaced them altogether; she only seemed ageless. She was born an Alton, Lew; she set her focus not in the minds, but in the living bodies of the Keepers. But her power was fading. Now she could not project her own form upon their bodies; she could only control their minds. And even that power was waning now. She would have done anything for a new source of power..."

Dio gasped, then pulled herself together a little.

"I was to be Keeper—I could sense it, a little, how horrible it was, what she wanted. I begged Lerrys to take me away to Vainwal. Why do you think I threw myself at you? I came to love you, but at first, I only wanted to be unfit for her!" Even her hands burned on mine.

"So it was Callina. But—sometimes Ashara had to withdraw, or Callina would have burnt out. Then Callina was normal, or else she was in trance. When I knew that Regis would have to use the Sword, I—went to the Tower, and smashed one of the crystals. That trapped Ashara for a little while. I had been trained a little, when they thought I was to be the Keeper, and I knew what to do, but I couldn't do it in my own body, because—" Again her cheeks flooded with color. "Callina, at least, was a virgin. Callina was in trance, and the Terrans had drugged her. So I went to Regis, and he used his Gift, and—and switched me into Callina's body. It was I who linked with you and Regis."

"No," I gasped, "No, it was Callina, Callina—"

Dio pressed herself to me, her arms around my neck. "No, my darling, no, Callina could not have linked in focus with you. She had not enough independent mind left. Lew, remember—you had never touched my mind, you gave me a barrier against you. And I knew that when it broke, we'd all be too overloaded to know whether I was Callina, or Dio, or someone else. And after that, the barriers were up again. But—darling—see?"

Suddenly she reached for me and went into complete rapport again. The familiar solace, sweetness, the cool and delicate warmth. "Callina!" I breathed.

No. This is the part of me you never knew....

Even now the rapport was too intimate to hold for long.

"In the old days, Lew—before you left Darkover—Callina was a lovely girl, sweet and generous and brave. You know that. She risked her life for you. But Lew, the real Callina died when Ashara took her. Days ago. She was already only a shell of herself, but oh, Lew, the bravery, the wonderful bravery of that poor, poor girl!" Dio was sobbing like a child. "Lew, she loved you. She refused rapport with you—before Ashara—because she knew it would have given Ashara a foothold in your brain and body, too. With her last spark of will, she saved you from that—and it was the last thing she ever did. It was her death—her real death. You thought Ashara disappeared? No; she had only overshadowed Callina. You thought Callina acted strangely on Festival Night? No. She was only—"

"Don't, don't tell me any more!" I begged.

"Only one thing more." She touched the still-discolored bruise on her cheek. "Why do you think I didn't try to stop Dyan—warn Callina against Derik? Lew, it was a desperate chance, but if they'd succeeded, it would have played into our hands. If a man—any man—had taken Callina, even in rape, so soon after Ashara had taken over her body, it would have caused enough disruption to drive Ashara out. It might have killed Callina, but there was a bare chance that it would have *freed* her, instead. Ashara would have had to withdraw, not for a few minutes, but permanently."

"Don't!" I implored, sick with horror.

"I tried to save Callina myself—" Dio broke off. "Oh, Lew, didn't it mean anything that Callina came to you that night, and slept in your arms? Callina was in trance, and I—I knew Ashara could drive me out of her body any minute, but I knew you wanted Callina, and I hoped—"

"Oh, Dio!" In spite of my horror, I began weakly to laugh; the first step of the long healing. "Dio, my darling love, *don't you ever look in a mirror?* By the time you reached my rooms, it *was* you again—in your own body! And Callina would have known I could not—" Suddenly, violently, I caught her to me, kissing the flaxen hair and the wet face. "Darling, darling, I'm going to have to explain a lot of things to you about matrices and the men who work with them!"

Crying and laughing at once, she raised her eyes. "But if it was me, me myself—then—Lew, you love me?"

Over her head my eyes blurred. *Callina!*

Her gray-green eyes, shorn forever of mischief, met mine tenderly. "I'm not Callina anymore," she said gravely, "but I'm not Ashara either. I think you're cured, Lew. If not, I too am damned."

I kissed her, and it was an exorcism for the past and an oath for the future. But I shut my eyes to the rising sun over her shoulder, knowing that forever I would walk with doubt, and face the sun with troubled eyes.

Abruptly the dawn was shattered with a burst of noise; Rafe and Regis ran into the courtyard.

"Lew," Rafe shouted harshly. "Come quickly! They've found Marja, alive!"

I let Dio go. Regis said, breathlessly, "Dyan had her under the matrix, and it blanked her like death; so he hid her the one place on Darkover where we would never look! When the matrix smashed, she went into shock, but there's a bare chance—"

Rafe grabbed my arm. "We've got a rocket-car."

We all crowded in, Rafe driving. The jets roared and we jerked back wildly as it screamed through a long curve and rammed back along the roadway not meant for these Terran inventions, horses and people fleeing in panic as we raced through the streets of Thendara.

Regis shouted, "When she collapsed, they called the Medical service at the HQ, and Lawton—"

Lawton, I thought, must be raving crazy by now, with first Thyra, then Kadarin, then Callina—Callina?—and me disappearing. But I could not worry about him now. We roared into the Terran Zone.

The streets were wider here, and the jets screamed as we slammed around corners still lighted with the neons of the night. We swept, in a wild slipstream of noise, into open country, and only minutes later we shrilled to a bone-shaking stop.

The sign read: THE READE ORPHANAGE FOR THE CHILDREN OF SPACEMEN.

Rafe banged on the door and a tall woman, prim-faced, in Terran garments, looked out at us. Rafe demanded, "Where is Marguerhia Kadarin?"

"Captain Scott? How did you know? Your niece is very ill; we were going to send for her guardian. Where is he?"

"You can't," I cut in. "He's dead. The child's in shock. I'm a matrix tech, lady; let me in."

Her eyes narrowed with suspicion and dislike at my crumpled Terran clothing, put on days ago to ride to the *rhu fead*; bloodstained; my unshaven face, my mutilated arm. "I'm afraid I must say—no visitors."

Another female voice interrupted. "Miss Tabor, can you keep the hallway quiet? Remember we have a very sick child—" She broke off, looking at the four of us. Only Rafe was presentable. "Who are these people?"

"I'm Marja's father," I begged. "Believe me, every second we stand here, we're losing what little chance—" Suddenly, with almost a prayer of thanks, I remembered the Terran cert card I had stuck into the pocket of this suit, the day I came to Darkover. I dived into the pocket. "Here. This will identify me."

She barely glanced at the plastic chip. "Come along," she said, and led me along the hallway. "We had to take her out of the dormitory. The other girls were frightened."

The room was small and clean and full of sunlight. Marja was lying in a high-sided crib, and Dr. Forth, from the Terran HQ, raised his head as I walked in.

"You? Did you say you know about this sort of thing?"

"I hope so," I said tonelessly and bent over her. My heart stopped. It was like looking at a dead child, one who has slept and slept and died sleeping. She lay slack on one side, her small hands limp and open, her mouth loose, breathing shallow and just audible. A single vein beat blue in her temple.

I frowned, making a tentative effort to touch her mind. No use. She was deep in trance; her mind was simply not in her body at all, and now even her body was failing.

No man can work among matrices without knowing all about shock-trance and how to cure it—if a cure is still possible. "Have you tried—" I named off a list of common restoratives, even though I knew that a child so young might not respond to treatment at all. It was almost unheard-of for a child to have any telepath ability. I had never heard of a precedent for this.

And if it were to be much longer, she might better not return at all, for she would be too changed.

The sun had crept high and was burning through the glass. I straightened finally, sweat dripping down my face, and said wearily, "Where are Regis and Dio—the boy and girl who came with me? Get them."

They came in, softly, and stopped, appalled, looking down at the limp Marja. I said, despairingly, "It's a last resort. We were in rapport with a matrix almost identical to Sharra." When Sharra smashed, and the Gate was shut, everyone sealed to Sharra was flung into that world—except me. I had been held to this world by a power stronger still. There was a chance we could still reach Marja with a triple touch. Her body was here, and that was a powerful tie. I had fathered that body, and that was another. But she could not force her way back alone.

"Regis. Can you hold me if I go out after her?"

His eyes held momentary dread, but he did not hesitate. Dio stretched a hand to both of us and for the last time that threefold consciousness locked between us; an extension of myself which went outward, farther and farther, through spaceless, timeless distance.

Shadows flickered, cold and malign. Then something stirred there and fluttered, something twitched drowsily away from my touch; something dreaming, happy, unwilling to wake—

Swiftly, with a harsh roughness that made Dio sob aloud, I smashed the fourfold rapport and caught Marja in my arms, with the feverish relief after deathly despair.

"Marja!" I heard my own voice, husky, broken, "Marja, precious, wake up!"

She stirred in my arms. Then her lashes fluttered and she smiled, sleepy and sweet, up at me.

"*Chi' z'voyin qui?*" she murmured drowsily.

I don't know what I said. I don't know what I did. I suppose I behaved like any man half crazy with relief. I know I hugged her till she whimpered; then I sat down, cradling her in my lap.

She pouted, "Why is ev'body looking at me?" And, as I tried to speak through my choked throat, she complained pettishly, "I'm *hungry*!"

In sudden, weak reaction, I realized I hadn't eaten for two days. I felt an almost insane relief at the chance to end this whole thing on a note of the most ridiculous anticlimax.

"I'm hungry too, *chiya*," I said weakly. "Let's all go and find you something to eat."

"And that," said Dio, lifting Marja easily by her little nightgown, "is the first sensible thing you've said since you came back to Darkover. Let's all go and eat. Matron, will you find this child some clothes?"

Two hours later, washed and fed and clothed, we made a respectable group around Lawton's desk in the HQ. He waved a spaceform at me.

"This just came over the relay," he said, and read it aloud. "'Abandon leads on Darkover. Katherine Marshall discovered on Samarra, slight amnesia, unharmed. Haig Marshall.'

"Allowing for the time lags in the relay," he said grimly, "she turned up on Samarra about half an hour after I talked to her here. Times, I'm tempted to throw up this job and turn spacehand." He looked at Regis' white hair; at Dio; at Marja, sitting in my lap. "You owe me an explanation, Lew Alton."

I looked back, gravely. I liked Dan Lawton. Like myself, he was a child to two worlds; but he, too, had chosen his path, and it was not mine. "Perhaps I owe you that," I said, "but it is a debt I fear that you will never collect."

He shrugged, tossing the spacegram form into a basket. "So I'll always have something coming. We've got to talk, anyway. Darkover's years of grace are over."

I nodded in slow agreement. The Comyn had won against Sharra, but it had lost, too.

"I got word from GHQ; I'm to start setting up a provisional government here, under Hastur—the Regent, not the kid. Hastur's sound, and honest, and the people trust him."

I agreed. The Hasturs had been the strength of the Comyn for generations; Darkover would be better off without the rest of us.

"You, young Regis, will probably come after him. By the time you're your grandfather's age, the people will be psychologically ready to choose your own rulers. Lew Alton—"

"Count me out," I said shortly.

"You have your choice. Exile—or staying and helping to keep things in order."

Regis turned to me, earnestly. "Lew, the people need Darkovan leaders, too. Someone who'll work wholly on their side. Lawton will do the best he can, but he's been Terra's man, all his life."

I looked sorrowfully at the young Hastur. Perhaps that was where he belonged. Ruler, even a figurehead; working for Darkover, stemming the tides of Terra as best one man could. Perhaps I belonged at his side.

"Won't you help me, Lew? We can do so much together!"

He was right. But all my life I had walked between two worlds, accused by each of belonging to the other. Neither would ever trust me.

"If you go, it's for good," Lawton warned. "Your estates will be confiscated. And you won't be allowed to come back. We don't want any more Kadarins!"

The words hurt, with their truth. That was the flaw in the Comyn. Misguided patriotism, self-sufficiency, the lack of some steadying balance—perhaps just the inability to see good in an enemy.

But I was Comyn. I had not asked to be born so, but I could not change. I looked away from the entreaty in Regis' eyes. "No," I said, "we'll go. I only want three things. Can I have 'em?"

"Depends," said Lawton. "I hope so."

I took Dio's hand. "To be married by our own people before we go," I said quietly, "and to straighten out the adoption papers on Marja. She's mine. But there are some mixed—"

He put out a hand to stop me. "Good God, let's not get tangled up in those weird family relationships again! Yes, I'll arrange it, unless—" he glanced at Rafe, but Rafe shook his head, a little regretfully.

"What could I do with a kid? It would just be the orphanage again." Lawton nodded. "What else?"

"A passport to clear space for four people." Four; Andres would not care to see the Terrans take over, I thought, even though it was the only right and logical way to end the story of the Comyn.

Regis asked, "Where will you go?"

I looked at the steady courage in Dio's eyes. I knew where I wanted to go and what I wanted to do, but could I ask it of Dio? Undecided, I looked at her. After all, I had lands and a heritage on Terra, which I could claim, and live there at ease.

Marja wriggled on my lap, clambered down and ran to Dio. She laid her mop of curls on Dio's shoulder, and Dio put both arms around her, and suddenly I made up my mind.

Halfway across the Galaxy there were pioneer worlds, where the name of Terra was a vague echo and Darkover a name unknown. There went all those who could find no place in the static Empire world, those who longed for a place outside the stylized universe of today.

If the Empire ever came so far, it would not be in our lifetime.

I went to Marja and Dio and circled them both with my arms.

"The farther, the better," I said.

Lawton glanced at me. For a moment I thought he would protest. Then he changed his mind, smiled in his friendly, reserved way, and rose. Regret and farewell were in the gesture.

"I'll arrange that, too," he said.

Three days later we were in space.

Darkover! Bloody sun! What has become of you? My world is fair, but at sunset there are times when I remember the towers of Thendara, and the mountains I have known. An exile may be happy, but he is an exile, no less. Darkover, farewell! You are Darkover—no more!

Also by Marion Zimmer Bradley

Darkover
Rediscovery
The Heirs of Hammerfell
The Planet Savers
The Sword of Aldones
Sword of Aldones

Darkover Anthology
The Keeper's Price
Sword of Chaos
Free Amazons of Darkover
The Other Side of the Mirror
Red Sun of Darkover
Four Moons of Darkover
Domains of Darkover
Renunciates of Darkover
Leroni of Darkover
Towers of Darkover
Marion Zimmer Bradley's Darkover
Snows of Darkover

Watch for more at www.mzbworks.com.

Made in the USA
Las Vegas, NV
26 February 2023